"We make arranged merger, yes?" Jafar Patel smiled at Annabelle. "I bring my son Kabir. In India, his name means *great.*"

Annabelle smiled at the young man standing next to Jafar. "It's a pleasure to meet you Kabir." He was looking at her with an eagerness that was unmistakably interest in her as a female, not a business partner. She mentally brushed him off and focused back on Jafar. "So, shall we sign the papers?"

"Merger first." Jafar continued to smile. "You and Kabir merge first."

What did Kabir have to do with anything? She had been negotiating with Jafar. "She shook her head. "I don't understand."

Jafar brought his hands together. "Merge." He took Kabir's hand and held it out. Kabir turned his palm upward.

"You mean introduction?" Of course. She placed her hand in his, then jerked it back when his grasp began closing over her fingers.

"Marriage."

"You mean merger?" Was he still confusing the two words?

JUST HAPPENED

Love Again

Falling Again

Just Stay

Just Chance

Just Believe

Just Us

Just Once

Just Happened

Just Maybe

Just Pretend

Just Because

JUST HAPPENED

THE WORTHINGTONS

KATHRYN KALEIGH

JUST HAPPENED

PREVIEW JUST MAYBE

Copyright © 2022 by Kathryn Kaleigh

All rights reserved.

Written by Kathryn Kaleigh

Published by KST Publishing, Inc., 2022

Cover by Skyhouse24Media

www.kathrynkaleigh.com

No part of this book may be reproduced in any form or by any electronic or mechanical means, including information storage and retrieval systems, without written permission from the author, except for the use of brief quotations in a book review.

This is a work of fiction. Any names, characters, places, or incidents are products of the author's imagination and used in a fictitious manner. Any resemblance to actual people, places, of events is purely coincidental or fictionalized.

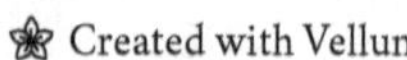 Created with Vellum

To learn more about Kathryn Kaleigh, visit

www.kathrynkaleigh.com

Kathryn Kaleigh

Scan me!

CHAPTER 1

*A*nnabelle Lawson put the cap on her thick highlighter and huffed out a breath at the long yellow streak across the paper. She would have to print a fresh copy when she got to the hotel. She leaned back in the leather seat and braced herself for the next air pocket. There was never just one.

She stared out at the checkerboard of fields below and wondered who the new pilot was. It seemed like every time she flew with Skye Travels Noah had hired someone new. His company was growing like gangbusters, seemingly with little effort on his part.

Of course, Annabelle knew firsthand that a company never grew without considerable effort.

Unfortunately, hers was suffering. A new medical waste removal company had come into Houston and had all but shut Steri-Waste down. Annabelle didn't care so much about the company, but it had been started by her grandfather, Nathaniel, so she was determined to save it. Besides, Steri-Waste had funded her college and kept her from having to worry about money.

The plane dipped into the inevitable air pocket and Annabelle gasped. She preferred flying with Samuel, but he worked with Noah at Skye Travels now. So she now flew with Skye Travels. Unfortunately, Samuel was out with the birth of his first child, so Annabelle had been forced to fly with another pilot.

Noah assured her that he was top-notch, but she was having doubts. Samuel always went around the turbulent weather. She closed her eyes. In all fairness, she knew that wasn't always possible. She was just miffed at having to fly with someone new. She'd met the copilot, Beau, but she'd yet to meet her pilot. In fact, from her seat, she could see Beau, but not her pilot.

She really just wanted to get this meeting over with. Over and done. She'd read all the paperwork, had her attorney double-check the contract, and was ready to just sign and get on with other things. Steri-Waste kept her at her standard of living, but more importantly her mother relied on the income. Her parents' divorce had been bad. The brutal divorce coupled with her father's floundering oil company, had left her mother relying on the Steri-Waste income. Unfortunately, it wasn't something that held Annabelle's interest.

But as executor of her grandfather's estate, it was just one of her many responsibilities.

She was anxious to get started on next venture – a publishing business. Publishing was something she could get excited about. Medical waste. Not so much.

CHAPTER 2

*B*randon Barrett made a swing around Mackinac Island for his own pleasure. He'd heard so much about the island. *Somewhere in Time* was his sister's favorite movie of all time and she'd spent her honeymoon on the island during some kind of *Somewhere in Time* festival. He didn't know the details, but his sister was intrigued as was her new husband.

He hit the Mackinac Island Airport runway at a perfect angle if he did have to say so himself. It was a short runway to begin with and the plane barely squeezed within the limits the runway could handle.

Feeling rather pleased with himself, he got up to see what kind of passengers he had on board. He'd already been in cockpit when they came in and his copilot, Beau, was taking care of everything in the back.

He stood up, stretched, and turned around to the empty cabin. Surely he didn't fly all the way up here with no passengers. Beau hadn't said much, but both of them were preoccupied with their own things. He went to the door and was about to call out to Beau.

Then he heard someone moving about.

He turned and saw her standing up and moving into the aisle.

His heart rate ramped up to full force. She was the most beautiful creature he'd ever seen.

She wasn't smiling. In fact, when she looked up and saw him, she scowled.

He'd just made an amazing landing and she wasn't showing any signs of being grateful. None whatsoever.

She put her handbag strap over her head and gathered up her leather briefcase. She was wearing a charcoal gray skirt and matching jacket. She had on a forest green blouse beneath it. As she walked toward him, he saw that she wore a silver chain that sparked with about four tiny diamonds around her neck and diamond studs on her earlobes. Her blonde-highlighted hair was loosely swept off her face. He also noticed that instead of the traditional business heels, she wore flat lace up booties.

One of the side effects of having a sister was learning to notice such details. As she neared him, he noticed a light scent of sandalwood and gardenia. His stomach clutched as he became acutely aware of her delicate femininity.

He smiled and asked his standard question. "How was your flight?"

"Rather bumpy, don't you think?" She gave him a half smile as she walked past him. Beau was there to help her down the steep steps to the ground.

Brandon rolled his eyes. She really knew how to crush a man's ego.

As he watched her walk toward the waiting car, he smiled.

Beauty with an edge.

CHAPTER 3

"We make arranged merger, yes?" Jafar Patel smiled at Annabelle. "I bring my son Kabir. In India, his name means *great.*"

Annabelle smiled at the young man standing next to Jafar. "It's a pleasure to meet you Kabir." He was looking at her with an eagerness that was unmistakably interest in her as a female, not a business partner. She mentally brushed him off and focused back on Jafar. "So, shall we sign the papers?"

"Merger first." Jafar continued to smile. "You and Kabir merge first."

What did Kabir have to do with anything? She had been negotiating with Jafar. "She shook her head. "I don't understand."

Jafar brought his hands together. "Merge." He took Kabir's hand and held it out. Kabir turned his palm upward.

"You mean introduction?" Of course. She placed her hand in his, then jerked it back when his grasp began closing over her fingers.

"Marriage."

"You mean merger?" Was he still confusing the two words?

When they'd begun their negotiations six months ago, he used the words interchangeably for awhile, but stopped when she continued to say *merger*.

His smile disappeared. "Not merger. Marriage." He pulled a diamond ring out of his pocket and handed it to his son.

Annabelle's stomach dropped. "No." She shook her head. "I can't."

"Marriage required for merger."

"I can't." Annabelle needed to sit down.

"But you want the deal, right?" Jafar stood there holding the ring in one hand, his other hand on Kabir's arm.

CHAPTER 4

$\mathcal{B}$randon sat within earshot of the little meeting. They sat on the porch of the Grand Hotel, supposedly the longest porch in the world. The view of the lake from here was breathtaking. The light afternoon breeze kept the temperature perfect. He wasn't sure why Annabelle Lawson had chosen to come here to meet with some Indian men, but surely she had a good reason. Perhaps they had requested the location.

They didn't know he was there. He'd been seated on a couch behind a planter spilling over with red geraniums when they'd met on the porch. If he understood them correctly, they were pressuring Annabelle to marry the younger man.

As her pilot, he felt some responsibility for her. Perhaps this was Noah's influence, but when he flew passengers to a location he stayed with them until they were ready to fly back. He tried to make sure they were taken care of. They often invited him to dinner with them and other social events, but even when they didn't he typically knew where they were and stayed in the same hotel.

As a result, he'd had some interesting experiences. He'd

escorted drunken passengers to their rooms, straightened out hotel reservations, and one time he'd even taken a guy to drop off one girlfriend and pick up another – at the same airport. That had involved tipping a line crew guy to scurry one girl out in a car while the other was coming out.

"I can't," Annabelle said.

"But we talked about the merger and you agree."

"I thought you meant business merger, not marriage."

As Brandon listened to the conversation, it was becoming more and more clear that this was a major misunderstanding. The business man wanted her to marry his son. Obviously, they'd only just met. And Annabelle wanted a merger, not a marriage.

He rubbed his palms against his eyes. He was a sucker for a damsel in distress. No way he could change that now.

He stood up and went to join the meeting. "Annabelle." He put his arm around her shoulders in a familiar hug. The top of her head came just to his shoulders. "I've been looking everywhere for you."

She glanced at him with a slight smile. "You're late."

He grinned. She was quick. He'd give her that. A little prickly, but quick on her feet. Unfortunately, he was pretty sure she didn't know his name.

CHAPTER 5

A wave of relief shot through Annabelle at having this conversation interrupted by someone she knew – the handsome pilot from her earlier flight. Relief was promptly followed by a mix of guilt and anxiety. She hadn't exactly been all that friendly toward him. In fact, she'd been uncharacteristically unfriendly. Critical even. And… for him to put her conversation with Jafar on pause, she needed to know his name – but she couldn't have told them if her life depended on it. She had paperwork, but it was in the room.

She took a deep breath. She could work with this. "Beau," she said, placing a hand on his chest. A very firm study chest. He wasn't wearing his uniform now. He'd changed into a pair of jeans and a pink Psycho Bunny shirt.

The pilot held out his hand and introduced himself. "Hello. I'm Brandon Beau Barrett. Most people call me Brandon."

"It's a pleasure to meet you Brandon Beau."

Annabelle smiled and swallowed her gaff. He could have just gone along with her. It wasn't like they were ever going to know any different.

"I'm Jafar and this is my son Kabir."

"Shall we sit down?" Brandon asked, ushering them all to a nearby table.

Annabelle had reserved a meeting room for them, but the porch was all but deserted. This would work just as well. Brandon held her chair while she sat and then sat next to her. Jafar sat on her other side and Kabir across from her.

Jafar watched them closely. "What is your relationship?"

Annabelle opened her mouth to answer, but she wasn't sure what to say. She glanced sideways at Brandon.

He immediately picked up the baton. "I'm her fiancé."

CHAPTER 6

*A*nnabelle felt a little hitch in her breath. She'd expected him to say *friend* or perhaps *boyfriend* at the most. But he'd jumped right in there with fiancé.

She kept her expression blank.

Jafar glanced at her hand. "No." He creased his forehead. "You did not mention this during our negotiations."

"Because I thought you just meant a business merger." Why was he not getting this? And how could this possibly be happening?

"I see." Jafar folded his arms.

Brandon pulled her close and kissed her hair above her temple. Little tendrils shot through her body. Though he'd changed clothes, he still smelled a little like jet fuel. When did jet fuel become sexy?

"Why do you not wear the customary ring on your finger?"

Annabelle found that she was getting her bearings. "We're trying to keep it a secret. My father wants me to marry someone else."

Jafar stroked his chin. "I see…"

"Only someone with Annabelle's beauty would have this problem." Brandon grinned. "I'm very fortunate."

"When is the wedding?"

"We don't have a date."

"December."

Annabelle and Brandon spoke at the same time.

Jafar smirked. "No. I don't believe you." He gestured toward his son. "I think you are merely trying to avoid marrying my son."

Annabelle scoffed. "Kabir is a very handsome man. But you know that arranged marriages aren't our custom."

"And mergers without gain aren't ours."

CHAPTER 7

Fiancé? Where had that come from? Brandon kicked himself. It would have been so much more logical to have just said boyfriend. But in his defense, they had been talking to her about marriage. At least he hadn't claimed to be her husband.

Though at the moment, that may have gone further to solve their problem.

Jafar obviously didn't believe that they were engaged. He'd already tripped them up on the wedding date. If he started asking more questions, it would become even more evident that they knew nothing about each other.

"What brings you to Mackinac Island?" It was time for Brandon to use his skill of distraction.

"Kabir is looking to purchase property here."

"A house?" According to Brandon's sister, it was virtually impossible to find someone selling a house on the island, especially a house with a lake front view.

"Yes. He will buy a house."

"Have you found one for sale?"

Jafar shrugged. "Not for sale, but when he makes his choice, he'll make an offer."

So this family had enough wealth to buy someone out of their home? Or so they seemed to think. No doubt these homes had been in families for generations. And Brandon knew firsthand that the longer property was in a family, the less likely it was to be sold. For any price. "Why here?"

"It is beautiful view." Jafar waved his arms. "And centrally located in America."

Brandon read between the lines. Kabir was looking for a green card. Or his father was looking for a green card for his son. Either way, Annabelle had no business being caught up in this. "My love, maybe we should talk about this. In private."

Annabelle smiled sweetly. "We have talked about it sweetie. And we agreed that this was the best thing for the family."

"Yes, but Jafar has added complications to the deal that we didn't prepare for." He turned to Jafar. Annabelle could yell at him later for hijacking her meeting. Right now he just wanted to get her out of this mess. "What other option would you consider?" Besides, they would expect the man to be the more logical one.

Jafar shook his head. "I see no other options. This was the deal we agreed upon."

"There was obvious miscommunication."

"Perhaps if I believed that you are engaged, I would be willing to consider other options."

"What can we do to convince you?" Annabelle asked.

"There's a chapel here, yes? Marry now."

CHAPTER 8

*A*nnabelle felt the floor drop out from beneath her feet. He wanted her to marry now? To marry someone she'd only just met? She hadn't even known his name until mere minutes ago. She was certain Jafar could see right through them.

Why would Brandon come to her rescue like this? They did need to talk in private. But right now, she just needed to find a way out of this.

"Weddings take months to plan. Families have to be present. We can't just up and have a wedding."

"Not wedding. Elopement. Elopements require no planning. You can have big wedding later with your family. What's not to like? You are here in perfect honeymoon spot. It's very romantic to have secret wedding."

Was the irony not lost on this man? He was suggesting that they have a secret romantic wedding. The same man who wanted her to marry his son as part of a business arrangement. His son whom she'd know less time than she'd known Brandon. Not that that was saying anything. "No. That would be improper."

"Very well." Jafar waved his hand. "If you change your mind, we will be in the hotel for four days. Until then the merger is off."

Annabelle watched in disbelief as Jafar and Kabir stood up and walked away.

As they entered the hotel and were out of sight, Brandon touched her shoulder.

"What?" She jerked and faced him.

"What is this about? How did you get into this mess?"

She looked toward the lake, the waves gently rolling in. Mackinac Island Island had always been one of her favorites. She, too, had thought about buying a house here. But, one, she really couldn't justify it right now. She'd probably barely use it. And two, there was never anything available. Unlike Jafar, she didn't have the disposable income to offer someone three or four times the market value of a house.

How did she get into this indeed? "Would you get me a mimosa?"

CHAPTER 9

$\mathcal{B}$randon turned his own question on himself as he went in search of a bar to buy Annabelle a drink. He'd gotten himself into this. Now he had to get himself out.

The man was insane. He wanted him to marry Annabelle. Brandon was certain she was a nice girl and probably would make a good wife, but the man's demand to see this wedding made no sense at all. There was something Annabelle wasn't telling him. A missing link to tie all this together.

He found a bar and ordered a mimosa for her and a martini for him. The bartender brought his drink first. He finished it off while they made the mimosa and he order a second to take back with him. As he walked the distance back to their table, he appreciated the historical ambiance of the hotel. He could see why his sister was enamored with it.

Personally, it was a little crowded for him. Brandon preferred sleek modern lines of the newer hotels. He never stayed at a bed and breakfast when he could stay at a hotel.

When he reached their table, at least what he was pretty sure was their table, she was not sitting there. *Great.* He shrugged and sat down. Stretched out his legs. It wouldn't be so bad to have to drink both of their drinks. He had two days before they were flying back.

He would disentangle himself from this whole thing and enjoy the rest of his trip. This was her mess and he'd listen, assuming she showed back up. But he knew better than to get enmeshed in a client's problems.

He lifted his gaze and saw her silhouette at the porch railing. The breeze tousled her shoulder length hair around her face. Even from here, he could see the sadness in her expression. He longed to pull her close and soothe her sadness away.

This was not good. *Never get involved with a client.* He wasn't even sure where he first heard that advice, but nonetheless, it was a well known rule of thumb. Failed relationships and hook ups didn't lead to repeat business.

He sipped his martini. Untangle. Get out.

CHAPTER 10

Annabelle clicked off her phone and slipped it into her pocket. As the breeze whipped her hair across her vision, a single teardrop slipped down her cheek.

It was so beautiful here. And from here she could see the lake, it's waves chopping toward the shore. The island held so many fond memories. She'd spent countless summers here exploring the island with her grandfather. He said he was going to buy a house they'd fallen in love with as soon as it became available. It was a three story Queen Anne cottage with a wrap around porch and a tall tower on one side that resembled a light house. Time went on and it didn't open up. Then he got sick.

She wiped at her cheeks, then turned her back on the lake. The quintessentially handsome pilot named Brandon *Beau* Barrett was sitting with his legs stretched out, a drink in one hand, watching her. She smiled to herself at how he'd covered for her calling him by the wrong name.

He'd told Jafar that he was her fiancé. So obviously he'd overheard at least part of their conversation. She'd been on the verge of walking away from Jafar and his son before Brandon showed up to bail her out. Then she had allowed him to take point. Annabelle didn't mind relinquishing some of the responsibility. In fact, it had been a welcome respite. She'd been making all the decisions since her grandfather had passed away and left her executor of his estate.

She wanted to help her mother and to preserve her legacy, but sometimes she felt trapped. Sometimes she just wanted to get away from it all and let someone else make some of the decisions.

Unfortunately, she'd just spoken with her mother and hadn't been able to dash her hopes of this merger. It would solve so many of their worries about the future. She'd told her mother that the negotiations were still underway.

She leaned back against the railing and propped one foot up behind her. He had one good thing going for him. He'd been vetted by Noah Worthington. And Annabelle trusted Noah's judgment. Even if she was still disappointed that he hadn't sent Samuel to be her pilot today.

She needed to think this through, but it was possible that there was an easy solution to her whole problem with Jafar. She just had to decide if Jafar was the kind of man she wanted to do business with now that she'd met him. It was quite an unexpected development that he thought she would actually marry his son as part of their business deal. She didn't for a minute believe that he'd gotten the words *marriage* and *merger* mixed up. He was much too successful to make a mistake like that. There was more to this story than he wanted her to believe.

In the meantime, it had been awhile since she'd spent the evening with a handsome man without being required to talk about business.

Perhaps this whole thing with Jafar could wait until morning to figure out.

CHAPTER 11

$\mathcal{B}$randon sometimes wondered what it would be like to have to worry about what to do with millions. Or perhaps even billions. He spent a lot of time chauffeuring people around who doubtless had those enviable worries; however, he'd never been on the inside. His mother had worked two jobs just to help him pay for all the extra fees involved in him getting his pilot's license.

He'd repay her someday. Someway.

As Annabelle walked toward him, he remained calm on the outside, but inside, his heart was racing. He'd put himself out on a limb for her and he had no idea how she would react. And on top of that, he needed to untangle himself from her mess. He only hoped it wasn't too late.

"I thought you'd left," he said.

"Where would I go?" She sat in the chair next to him, her back straight, and picked up her mimosa.

He shrugged. "It's a big hotel."

"It is, isn't it?" Her eyes lit up. "I love it here."

So perhaps it wasn't Jafar who had picked the location of

their meeting. It was Annabelle. "Have you spent a lot of time here?"

She nodded. "Several summers ago when I was younger." Her voice was wistful, sad even. She sipped her drink, keeping her eyes down.

Brandon straightened. He wanted to know more. He wanted to know how she ended up here on Mackinac Island Island. He'd assumed she was from Texas. She had a Texas accent. And the top of Michigan was a world away. And not just Michigan, but a tiny little island off of Michigan. It was beautiful here, but how did anyone find this place to begin with?

She lifted her chin and gazed up at him then. Gazed up at him with beautiful green eyes. Any thoughts Brandon had were suddenly no longer in his head. All he saw was a beautiful, vulnerable young woman.

And he realized in that moment that it was already too late to untangle himself from her. Maybe it had been from the first time he saw her. Every instinct in his body moved into protective mode. He would do whatever he could to protect her.

Even if it meant marrying her.

CHAPTER 12

Annabelle forced herself to relax. Breathe in. Breathe out. Relax. This was not the time for a panic attack. "Can we talk about something else?" She blinked back the moisture that threatened to spill over.

Brandon looked perplexed. "Sure. What do you want to talk about?"

"I don't know. Anything."

Brandon grinned. "How about them Dallas Cowboys?"

She laughed and felt some of the tension fall from her shoulders. "Wow. A pilot who talks about something other than flying."

He tilted his head. Considered. "Are we really that bad?"

"Yes."

He chuckled. "Tell me more about what you do besides gather marriage proposals."

She rolled her eyes and blew out a breath. "Unfortunately, I'm more like you guys than I'd like to admit. I'm a little single minded as well."

"That's not always a bad thing."

"No. Not unless it's not what you really want to do."

"What is it you want to do?"

She'd never had anyone lead with that question. In fact, she was having a hard time remembering the last time anyone even asked her that question. "I want to start a publishing business."

"Publishing. Huh? Are you a writer?"

"Me? No." She shook her head and leaned back in her chair. "I'm a reader."

"Does anybody use a publisher anymore?"

"Sure. A lot of writers do. Especially writers just starting out that haven't made a name for themselves yet. As a publisher I can offer promotion that a writer typically can't afford."

"You would be the editor, too?"

"At least at first, I'll decide which books to accept. But I'll leave the actual editing to professional editors.

"It sounds like you have it all planned out."

She nodded. "I do. I just need to get some of this other stuff out of the way so I can focus on it."

And make sure my mother is taken care of before I invest in a new venture.

CHAPTER 13

*A*nnabelle was more complicated than Brandon had expected. On the outside, she had the classic conservative rich girl appearance. But on the inside, there was so much going on.

She'd just had a business merger – probably a major deal – go south and she didn't even want to talk about it. Then he learned that she'd practically grown up here – in Michigan – on this island and she didn't want to talk about that either.

But she did want to talk about her new publishing house. Her eyes lit up when she talked about it and some of the sadness seemed to wash away.

A woman this beautiful and this successful shouldn't have such a glaze of sadness.

What had happened to her? He wanted to know, but she was fragile and he didn't want to press her to talk about anything that might bring those tears back to her eyes.

She was an enigma. Somehow she'd managed to remain impassive during her business meeting, but now, with him, she was more transparent.

Perhaps that was a compliment. He wondered how many

people actually listened to her. To what she wanted. Not what she could do for them.

"It'll take a lot of time to read all those submissions."

"That won't be a problem. I read a lot anyway."

"What got you interested in publishing?"

"My grandfather," she said simply, lowering her eyes again.

"Yeah. Tell me about him."

The sadness returned to her features. "I'll tell you sometime." Her voice was soft.

"Sure." He reached out and placed his hand lightly over hers. He took it as a good sign that she didn't pull away.

Again, he felt that intense urge to protect her. He wanted to see the light return to her eyes. "What kind of books do you like?"

"I like all kinds, but I especially like paranormal. You know, vampires and such." She had an impish expression that he hadn't seen before.

He was enamored. "Is that what you intend to publish?"

"Probably. But I'll probably publish several genres."

He wanted to ask the difficult questions. Like what was holding her back from starting her publishing company. Was it money? Was it energy? What part did her grandfather play in all this? But he didn't ask. He maintained the small talk and allowed her to avoid the subjects that he wanted to know about.

For now.

CHAPTER 14

The plaintive wail of a horn signaled the departure of a ferry as it set off across Lake Huron. Seagulls cawed as they circled their way around the island, dipping here and there, riding free on the wind.

Annabelle could talk about her grandfather's business. She could tell people how he'd taught her everything she knew about running a company.

But talking about the grandfather she knew personally, the one who'd taught her everything from tying her shoes to instilling a love of commercial fiction – the kind English teachers would frown upon, caused a lump in her throat that could easily morph into a flood of tears. It didn't matter that it had been ten years ago. "I don't want to talk about me anymore. Tell me something about you."

"Well… I'm a pilot."

She blew out a breath. "That's a relief."

"I had you worried with the bumpy flight, huh?"

She smiled. "Sorry about that. I was just miffed that my usual pilot wasn't available."

"Which one is your usual pilot?"

"Samuel."

"Ah. Noah's son-in-law. Didn't he just have a baby."

"He did. He's been flying me around since I was a kid."

"I'm getting the feeling that your childhood wasn't typical."

"Ha. Not at all. But we're talking about you." She wanted distraction right now. Distraction from the weight on her shoulders.

"Right." He leaned back in his chair again, extending his long legs out and propping his feet on her chair rungs.

It was only her chair and he was only propping his feet, but it felt oddly intimate, despite the fact that he wasn't actually touching her. She recalled the feel of his strong chest when he'd pulled her close. She shifted and sat up a little straighter. Looked at him with a raised eyebrow.

"There's not much to tell." He had a smirk on his face as though he knew he was tipping the edge of propriety.

At twenty-three, Annabelle had never had a serious boyfriend. She hadn't had the time to give to a relationship. She'd dated, of course, but never to the point of engagement. The one boyfriend that she'd thought could have gone serious, accidentally tipped his hand about dating her only for her wealth. Apparently, he thought she had a lot of money. A lot more than she did. Then there was her teen crush on Samuel, but that was another story.

She scoffed. "I don't believe you. Anyone who jumps in and pretends to be a stranger's fiancé, couldn't possibly have had a boring life."

He laughed. "Pilots do tend to enjoy adrenalin."

It was beginning to make sense now. "So, you just thought you'd jump in and play a game." Annabelle's spirits deflated. Games were not her things. In fact, that was probably the reason she hadn't gotten married. At the hint of game playing, she was out.

Brandon was frowning now. "I wasn't playing. You seemed to be in a bad situation. I was trying to help out."

"Thank you." No one had ever seen her as a damsel in distress. Except maybe Samuel. It was an odd feeling – one that took her emotions down a new path. A path that had been closed off since her grandfather had passed away.

"All right." He leaned forward. "My name is Brandon Barrett. I'm from Dallas, Texas. I'm thirty-one years old. Never married. No children. Not currently in a relationship."

She stared at him blankly for a moment. He'd just spouted way more information than she'd expected. Personal information. Then she laughed.

And held out her hand. "It's a pleasure to meet you Brandon. I'm Annabelle."

He took her hand in his and anything else she was about to say evaporated from her brain. Instead of shaking her hand, he grasped it and held on tightly.

She didn't try to pull away. Instead he sat up, using her chair to slide his closer.

His lips curved at the corners, he concentrated his gaze on hers. She was mesmerized by the cool blue of his eyes. The firmness of his hand on hers, and his feet on her chair beneath her, she felt a little like a bunny about to be devoured by a fox.

But unlike the bunny, she was drawn to her self-destruction and wanted it very much.

CHAPTER 15

The breeze from Lake Huron drifted over them as the afternoon sun began its descent toward the horizon. Indiscernible conversations from other guests drifted over them, not settling into their attention.

Brandon wanted to devour her. Annabelle was an enigma. In one aspect, she was obviously a very successful business person. In other aspects, she exuded vulnerability. Vulnerabilities that she appeared reluctant to share, yet to Brandon they were right there in plain view. And pulling it together, she seemed to know which areas she was vulnerable in and kept herself from going to those places. Successful. Self-aware. Beautiful as sin.

And Brandon was intrigued by puzzles.

It was going to take time to peel back the layers of her complexity. He knew that if he could rein in his impatience to learn everything all at once, he had the time and patience to do so. And he wanted to. He wanted to see what was beneath the next layer. He wanted to know everything about her.

He was certainly no psychologist, but he knew enough about people to know that he had to open up first. He'd let his impatience get ahead of himself. He'd spilled out too much information at once. But he wanted her to know up front that he wasn't toying with her. He wasn't a married man looking for a dalliance. He knew the unfortunate stereotype about pilots. A girl in every port.

Brandon kept his head down and his nose clean. He'd been in a few serial relationships, but it took a different kind of girl to get into a relationship with a pilot. One who could trust and wasn't afraid to spend large chunks of time without him. Those girls were hard to find. Especially one that grabbed hold of his attention like Annabelle had.

"So…" She grinned impishly. "Are you gay?"

He burst out into laughter, but didn't let go of her hand. "No. I'm very heterosexual."

"Then tell me Brandon Barrett, why you're still single?"

"Actually, I'm engaged."

Her brow furrowed and she looked disappointed before she caught herself. "You said you weren't in a relationship."

"Right. I didn't want to say because I *might* be engaged."

"You're not very good at this."

He put his other hand over their clasped hands. "What is it I'm not good at?"

She shifted in her chair. "Whatever it is you're playing at. You don't seem to have your story straight."

Playing? Brandon was not a player. But obviously she had some experience in that area. Never a good thing.

"Maybe I'm a little confused myself. I don't remember you answering one way or another when I offered to be your fiancé."

CHAPTER 16

$\mathcal{A}$nnabelle bit her lip to catch a gasp. She'd thought that little charade was merely for the benefit of Jafar.

And now he'd brought it up again. When it was just them. "Right," she said. "I guess I didn't hear the question."

He chuckled, then patted her hand, released it, and sat back. He sat back and narrowed his eyes at her. "Your turn."

This was turning into a dangerous game. The laughter of the nearest guests, a little family, three tables over, filled the air with happiness. What could it hurt to play along just a little with him? After all, her life was in his hands when they were in the air. Noah knew exactly where she was, so it wasn't like Brandon would turn out to be a serial killer. "I'm twenty-three."

He nodded. "Husband? Children?"

"No." She shook her head and rubbed her hands together. She was suddenly chilled without him leaning close and holding her hand. She clasped her hands together and rested her chin on them.

"Never?"

She shook her head again and watched as a carriage pulled

up to the front of the hotel. Perhaps she would take a carriage down to the lake a little later. Maybe have dinner at the wharf.

It would make a lot more sense than going down this path with Brandon. He was merely toying with her. "I think I'll go to my room and get changed."

"Okay." Brandon sat up. "Do you have more meetings or are you free for the evening?"

"I'm free. No more meetings."

"What do you have planned?"

"Not much." She stood up. It would really be nice to change into jeans. "I might go downtown and get some dinner."

"What about here? I heard the restaurant is good."

"Too formal."

"Do you mind if I tag along? It's my first time on the island?"

"Seriously?" He wanted to hang out with her?

He shrugged. "If you don't mind the company."

She could walk around by herself or she could walk around with the handsome pilot. Not a very big choice. "I'll meet you back here in an hour."

CHAPTER 17

Brandon took a quick shower and slipped on a pair of jeans and a leather jacket. Since they weren't eating at the formal hotel, surely she intended to go someplace less formal. A place where jeans would be okay.

He was ready in twenty minutes, so he spent some time wandering around the hotel. He found a bar, the Cupola Bar, on the fourth floor with grand views. Perhaps he'd come back here later with Annabelle.

Annabelle. She was all he could think about. He found her both beautiful and interesting. She smelled like magnolia blossoms and vanilla. Her features were delicate and her hair was soft. He'd wanted to kiss her and it had taken all his restraint not to.

He wasn't sure what he was going to do about her. He had kind of put himself out there claiming to be her fiancé. He hadn't mentioned it, but surely she knew they had to keep up the appearance of being a couple while they were on the island. If not, it would give Jafar more reason not to believe their story. And more reason to try to pressure her into marrying his only son in order to close a deal. What kind of deal could be so important that she would even consider marriage to a stranger? Especially a stranger from India who barely spoke the language and had customs she wouldn't understand. Nor would he understand her or her customs.

He wound his way back to the grand porch and found a seat where he could watch the elevator for her to come back. He contemplated what he would say if Jafar saw him sitting there.

Part of him wanted the man to mind his own business, but another part, perhaps stronger, wanted to make sure Annabelle's best interests were taken into account. Even if it meant putting up with the ridiculous notions of the man.

A couple, hand in hand, walked past. Brandon was reminded that they were in one of the country's most romantic destinations. Not very well known, especially down south, but romantic nonetheless. It wasn't going to be a hardship to spend the evening with the lovely Annabelle. Even if she did seem to have issues of avoidance – with both talking about herself and trusting him.

What would she do about Jafar? He didn't know what was expected in a situation like this. Where he was from, a girl would have just told them to hit the road. But then he'd never known anyone with so much at stake, that this situation would even arise. The closest thing he could come up with was a shotgun wedding. And that was miles from what was going on here. Annabelle had probably never even heard of a shotgun wedding. Except maybe in the history books. On second thought, she did like to read.

With his thoughts going round and round, he almost didn't recognize her. Her shoulder-length hair fell loosely around her face. She wore jeans and a short leather jacket.

He grinned like a loon as he walked up and hugged her. "We match and we weren't even trying." He said against her ear, absorbing her delicious scent of magnolia and vanilla.

She patted his arm. "That happens sometimes when people get engaged."

He slid his hands down her arms and took her hand in his, turning. "I've never been engaged before, so I didn't know that."

She looked at him sideways. "You have so much to learn."

He laughed and held the front door open for her. "Our carriage awaits." They went to the first horse-drawn carriage and he held her hand to steady her as she stepped up. He then settled in beside her.

CHAPTER 18

Annabelle had ridden in the carriages on Mackinac Island countless times, but never with her senses so alive. The air smelled clean, with the scent of flowers mingled with fresh air from Lake Huron.

Her thigh was pressed against Brandon's as they sat side by side in the carriage. The driver sat silently in front of them.

"Have you decided what you're going to do?" Brandon asked. His voice was kind, not judgmental.

She watched two children swinging in the front of a white picket fence as they rode past. And wondered if they lived here during the winter. Annabelle had never been to Mackinac in the winter, but she'd always been intrigued by the idea. She imagined how nice it must be to have nothing to do all winter, but sit in front of the fireplace and read. To have no meetings and places she had to go. "Something will come to me." It always did.

"This merger must be really important."

She glanced at him. She hadn't wanted to talk about it. She just wanted to be away from business for a time. But somehow talking with him didn't feel like work. "It could be."

"That's a rather vague response."

"It has to do with my family business."

"I assumed it was something like that."

She smiled. Of course he did. Things always seemed simple to people who weren't involved. "It's complicated."

"It always is."

She laughed. Just as things always seemed simple to outsiders, things always seemed complicated to those on the inside.

"How long have you been running the family business?"

"Since I was eighteen. I was going to go abroad for a time, but instead, I stayed and went to college in Dallas so I could run the business."

"Wow. That's a lot to put on someone so young. Especially a college student."

"I was the only one who could do it."

"What about your parents?"

"My father had his own company and my mother couldn't care less about business. My grandfather just skipped over her and taught me everything. I think he always knew she didn't have a head for business."

"What does she do?"

"She's a socialite, I guess. Or she was. When she was married to my father. She doesn't do much of anything now. Tends her garden mostly."

"You're an only child then?"

"Yep. Just me."

"Doesn't sound too complicated. Just sounds like you had a lot dumped on you at an early age."

"It wasn't intentional. My grandfather..." She swallowed the lump in her throat that was always there when she spoke about him outside of business. "He got sick. He planned on bringing me into the business after I spent some time abroad and after I went to college." She turned away so he wouldn't see the moisture in her eyes.

They rode in silence then until they came to the downtown area. The driver stopped and they descended from the carriage. Before she could open her handbag, Brandon handed the driver money.

"I should pay for it. It's a business expense."

"It's a business expense for me, too." He winked at her. "Noah will make sure I get it back."

She shrugged. The downtown area was a little more crowded now. But not nearly as crowded as it would be on the weekend. "There's a little tavern over there that's good." She pointed across the street.

Once inside the tavern, they were immediately seated and a few minutes later, a burly man came out to their table. "Annabelle! Is that you?"

"Hi Mr. Stinger." She smiled. "How are you?"

"Good. Come on, give me a hug." He pulled Annabelle out of her chair and into a hug. "I'm sorry about your grandfather."

"How did you know?"

Mr. Stinger straightened. "He sent a letter. Told us to take care of you when you came back."

"Oh." Annabelle sat back down, feeling a little light-headed. Her grandfather had told people that he was ill, then? "I didn't know that."

"What can I get for you?" Mr. Stinger turned to Brandon. "For you and your friend."

"This is my friend, Brandon."

They ordered drinks and Mr. Stinger promised to send out appetizers on the house.

"You're well known around here." Brandon commented.

"I guess. It's been years since I've been here."

"It may have been, but you made an impression."

Annabelle didn't correct him. She didn't tell him that it was her grandfather who had made the impression.

CHAPTER 19

After the server brought out an artisan cheese plate, Annabelle ordered a grilled salmon salad with avocados and mandarin oranges. Brandon ordered pistachio Michigan whitefish. He ordered a beer and she ordered water.

The atmosphere here was relaxed and friendly. Only three other tables were filled, so it was quiet with only a hum of conversation.

Brandon tasted a little cheese cube and leaned back in his chair. It was a beautiful evening on a charming island and he was here with a beautiful girl. He couldn't ask for much more, except maybe to put a smile on the beautiful girl's face.

"What do you do for fun?" He asked.

"Read." She nibbled a bite of cheese. "What do you do?"

"Fly."

"That's your job."

He shrugged. "I'm fortunate to have a job that I love."

"I think I would enjoy my job in publishing. But really, what do you do when you aren't in the air?"

"I do some woodwork?"

"Really?" She leaned forward. "What kind of woodwork?"

"Well… I'm renovating my house. I gutted my kitchen and rebuilt everything."

"That's impressive. To be able to do something like that."

He nodded. "It's fun. I'm going to replace my floors next."

"Sounds like you're handy to have around."

He grinned. "I like to think so."

"So flying and renovating. Both sound like work to me. What about leisure time?"

"Netflix. Movies. But I have a feeling we both could use a little play time."

She looked at him sideways. "Probably."

There was that caution again. There had to be a way around it. "I was looking online at things to do here. While you're figuring out whether we're engaged or not, I was thinking that we could rent some bicycles and ride around the island tomorrow." He hesitated. Remembered that this was a business trip for her. "If you're not busy."

She smiled. And the smile lit up her green eyes - eyes framed with long dark lashes. "My meetings are a little delayed at the moment."

His heart rate tripped up a notch at the prospect of spending the day with Annabelle. At this moment, he could think of nothing he'd rather do.

"Let me sleep on it," she said, dashing his hopes. "I should have a better idea about what I'm going to do in the morning."

"Of course." He shifted his gaze away. And mentally kicked himself. She would see him as her driver. Her pilot. If she didn't have anything else to do, she might do something with him.

The server brought their entrees and they ate in silence for a few minutes. She only ate a few bites before putting down her fork. "I was thinking it would be nice to take a walk along the shore after dinner."

And just like that, his good mood returned.

CHAPTER 20

nnabelle picked at her salad. The grilled salmon was delightfully crusty and the added oranges gave the salad an added tanginess. Unfortunately, she was a little too preoccupied to enjoy it.

Usually one drink would take the edge off and she could relax, but it didn't seem to be working tonight.

Perhaps she was worrying too much. The thing with Jafar would work itself out. Business deals always did. But this thing with Brandon was another thing entirely.

She'd said she needed to sleep on her plans for tomorrow. The truth was, she needed to sleep on her attraction to him.

She'd spent enough time around pilots to know better than to get attached. The few she'd gotten to know over the years, Samuel being the exception, had a strong need for adrenalin. They liked to spent their off time playing hard. She didn't blame them. But she'd heard too many of their stories on their return trips. Love 'em and leave 'em. Never once had she heard a pilot say that he was going to pursue a relationship with a girl he'd met on a trip. Not once.

So she knew too much. And it wasn't just pilots. It was the

nature of travel. She'd implemented her own policy of staying to herself on trips. It was a sure way to stay out of trouble and avoid heartbreak.

Yet here she sat with the handsome pilot who'd given her a bumpy ride to the island. He would be the one to take her home and the return trip could potentially be long and painful. She needed to keep her distance.

He was looking a bit downcast at the moment. She hadn't exactly been very open at the idea of spending time with him. That was when she'd offered to take a walk with him. She'd planned to take a walk along the shore anyway, but since he was here and she enjoyed his company, it just made sense.

Besides, what harm could it do to just enjoy his company for awhile? It wasn't like she was going to fall in love and expect a relationship out of him.

She knew better than to allow that to happen.

She smiled at him and her heart skipped at the way his face lit up in response. He was dangerously handsome and he had a boyish charm that she was having a hard time resisting.

When the server brought the ticket, she snagged it before he did and gave the server her credit card. He just grinned at her.

Maybe it would be okay to just enjoy his company. Just for one evening.

What could it hurt, right?

CHAPTER 21

They started walking down Main Street right at the beginning of sunset – just as the sky exploded into bright colors. They followed the path along the shoreline, walking until the town gave way to houses along the shore.

They left the trail and walked down to the edge of the water and watched the waves gently lapping at the shore. A ferry headed out across the lake.

"How did you ever find this place?" Brandon asked.

"My grandfather had a good friend from college who lived in Cheboygan. I think he visited here during school breaks."

"Not exactly Daytona Beach."

She laughed. "No. But my grandfather didn't do anything like anyone else did. That's why he was a millionaire by age thirty."

"Interesting." He picked up a rock. Threw it into the lake. "So he had that entrepreneurial spirit."

"That's an understatement."

"Did you get that gene or do you just push yourself?"

She crossed her arms and stared at him. "No one's ever asked me that before."

He picked up another rock. Tossed it from one hand to the other. "I think it makes a difference, don't you?"

"I would say that it makes quite a bit of difference. But I'm not sure whether it's all that easy to tell."

"I'd say you have it."

"Yeah. What makes you think that?"

"Because when you talk about doing something else, you don't talk about hanging out at the beach being a bartender or traveling or even having kids and raising them." He swung his arm back and tossed the rock into the water. "Nope. You talk about starting a publishing business."

"Did you play baseball in your youth?"

"What?" He laughed. "No. But I did spend some time on the lake."

"Hmm. You've got a good arm. And hanging out on the lake counts as a leisure activity."

"Yeah. Well, I don't do that so much anymore." He took her hand they made their way back to the trail.

The trail was picturesque with the lake and sunset on one side and historic homes on the other.

Just as they seemed to be running out of civilization, Annabelle froze.

CHAPTER 22

In her youth, Annabelle had daydreamed about doing the very thing she was doing at this moment. Walking along the island's shore, holding a handsome man's hand. It was as though they were the only ones on the island. There were houses to their right, but either no one was home or they were ensconced inside.

It was the last house on the right. A tall white house with a three story lighthouse shaped wing on one side. This was the house that she and her grandfather had talked about buying. Someday. But it was never for sale and someday never came.

She stood frozen, pulling Brandon back to stand next to her.

"What's wrong?" He asked.

She could only shake her head. She held up a hand toward the house.

There sitting dead center in the front lawn was a *for sale* sign. "It's for sale," she whispered.

He stood next to her, still gripping her hand. She was aware of her hand in his. The way he stood a head taller with broad shoulders.

She swallowed and took a deep breath. She had to tell him now. She couldn't just stand here staring like a crazy person without an explanation. "This is the house we talked about buying."

"Who's that? Your grandfather?"

"Yes. Every time we walked past, we talked about how someday it would go up for sale. I think he even talked to the owner once when they were outside. It was a summer home for them and they were spending less and less time here because they were getting up in age. But then they must have had children who held onto it. He said as soon as it was for sale, he was going to buy it." She was surprised at how easy it was to talk about her grandfather to Brandon. "We would stay here during the summers."

"It's a beautiful house."

She nodded.

"Have you been inside?"

"No."

He tugged on her hand. "Let's go check it out."

"What?" She pulled back. "We can't just go knocking on their door.

"Why not? It says for sale by owner."

"I know, but I think you have to call first."

"It's Mackinac Island. How many calls do you think they get?"

"Not very many." She stood her ground.

"Trust me. If they want to sell, they'll be ecstatic that someone is interested."

"They'll think we're tourists."

"That's the chance they have to take. Even if we called first."

She allowed him to pull her forward up the little sidewalk, the porch, to stand at the front door."

Every ingrained instinct she had screamed at her that is was not the proper way to go about it.

But he was knocking on the door.

CHAPTER 23

*B*randon knocked a second time and looked around. There was a wicker porch swing painted in a deep green swaying in the breeze. He'd noticed that all the buildings on the island seemed to be decorated in bright, cheerful colors, despite the clean white exterior paint.

Annabelle hung back, standing at the top of the stairs. He turned and grinned at her. "I don't think anyone's home."

Just then the door opened. A middle-aged man greeted them. "Can I help you?"

"Yes," Brandon said. "We saw your for sale sign and were wondering if we could take a look around."

"Oh course. Come on in."

Brandon took her hand. "Come on. See. He doesn't mind."

Annabelle rolled her eyes, but followed him inside.

Again, bright, warm colors gave the house a friendly, relaxed feel.

"I'm packing some things up. By the way, my name is Sawyer Taylor. I inherited this place from my parents. I'm an attorney in Chicago and my wife's idea of a vacation is to visit the Florida Keys, so I can't hold onto this house."

"It must be hard to let it go," Annabelle said.

"It is. My parents loved it here. But this house needs someone who can actually use it. It doesn't deserve to sit here like this."

"I don't know if I could do that."

"When you have kids, it seems like everything changes. Sawyer led them to the back of the house to the kitchen."

"Do you two have kids?"

CHAPTER 24

Annabella admired the huge kitchen done in pastel blues with modern appliances in black. There was a little breakfast nook set off to the side and a wall of windows on the back. The backyard had freshly cut green grass. The room had a homey comfortable feel to it.

Sawyer's questions startled her. He'd assumed that she and Brandon were a couple. Brandon hadn't exactly said that they were or weren't. But he had taken her hand. That rather quickly knocked out the notion of siblings or even just friends.

Brandon jumped in. "No. Not yet. I have to get her to marry me first."

Sawyer laughed. "Well, she looks like a good one. Surely you can talk her into saying yes."

Annabelle felt the heat rise to her cheeks. People usually knew her as the CEO of Steri-Waste. She was rarely in a situation for ambiguity. Here she was just Annabelle. Brandon's girlfriend.

She found the whole thing rather… sexy.

Deciding on a whim to play along and throw the men off balance, she took Brandon's hand and batted her eyelashes at him. "That's hard to do when he hasn't asked me yet." She held up her bare left hand for Sawyer to see.

Sawyer cleared his throat. "Don't wait too long. It's been my experience that if you wait around too long, they just move along."

Brandon scowled at her, but she just smiled. "That's good advice if I ever heard it." She turned back toward the front of the house. "Is it possible to see the lighthouse part of the house?"

"Of course." Sawyer seemed relieved to get out of that situation. "Follow me."

Annabelle stepped into the round room and fell instantly in love. Instead of being separated into three stories like she'd expected, it was all one room. Windows on every side – three stories of them. It seemed to capture the sunset and bring it straight into the room gleaming over the white couch and chairs and the white rug on the hardwood floor. One of the windows was open and the fresh scent from the lake spilled into the room.

She turned in a circle, taking it all in. Then looked straight at Sawyer. "I absolutely love it."

Sawyer beamed. "You're making me not want to sell." He laughed.

"Brandon." She turned her gaze on him. "Don't you love it?"

CHAPTER 25

$\mathcal{B}$randon blinked. He was having a hard time focusing on the house with Annabelle standing there, focusing that smile of hers on him. "I do love it." He managed the words, then followed them upstairs.

Annabelle was in love with this house, but Brandon had just tripped and fallen head over heels for her.

He'd seen it coming. He'd just chosen to ignore it.

He'd had this happen one time before. When he was in sixth grade and he'd fallen at

Becky Boone's feet. They'd been in school together since first grade and he'd always liked her, but then one day, just out of the blue, she'd asked him a question. He didn't remember the question, he just remembered that sudden feeling that had enveloped him. He'd never told her and she'd moved away the next year.

He'd never thought of falling for her as being too odd because he'd known her so long. But he was never sure what happened in that moment.

And right now he felt like he'd been shot in the heart with

cupid's arrow. The feeling was so intense, it almost took him to his knees.

He stood at the top of the stairway as she went from room to room with Sawyer.

He had to be cool. He couldn't let her know that he'd fallen for her. She'd think it was just too weird.

Hell, he thought it was weird.

A few minutes later, they came back to the landing.

Annabelle was in deep conversation with Sawyer. "Would you be okay with us coming back tomorrow? I want to sleep on it, but I might want to make an offer."

CHAPTER 26

*A*nnabelle didn't mind making quick decisions if she was sure, but she also knew that a major decision should be at least be slept on. Her grandfather had impressed three rules on her. The first one was always sleep on it before making a big decision. The second was to treat everyone with kindness even if she had to fire them and the third was to follow her heart.

She'd always seen number one as a checks and balance for number three.

She turned her attention to Brandon. He didn't look so good. Maybe the thought of buying a house so impulsively bothered him. It would have bothered her, too, except that her immediate love of the house coalesced with years of admiring it from the outside and memories of talking with her grandfather about buying it. "We should go and let Sawyer get back to his packing."

"Come back anytime," he told them as he led them toward the front door.

"Are you okay?" She asked Brandon as they went down the

front steps. Dusk had set in and it would be dark by the time they got back to the hotel.

"Yeah." He answered, but he was staring straight ahead, his forehead creased in thought, with his hands jammed in his pockets.

"You don't look so good."

He shrugged. "I'll be okay."

Annabelle wasn't so sure about that, but she refused to let him put a damper on her good mood. Sawyer had her phone number and had agreed to call him if he had any offers on the house.

She felt like skipping in the moonlight, but, of course, she didn't. A sense of decorum was far too ingrained. So instead, she let her imagination play. She could run her publishing business from here. Everything was online now, so location didn't matter. It would be a huge lifestyle change from her life of lattes and business suits. One that she found herself dreaming about more times than she liked to admit. Especially when sitting in rush hour traffic in Dallas. There was certainly no rush hour traffic here on the island.

Her phone buzzed pulling her out of her fantasy world.

It was a text message from her mother.

And everything came crashing back to earth. If she didn't complete this merger with Jafar, she wouldn't have the money to buy this house.

CHAPTER 27

$\mathcal{B}$y the time they had walked back down the trail to the town, Brandon had pulled himself together to make the conscious decision that he was going to think about his unusual reaction to Annabelle. He needed to be present at the moment, especially since whatever text message she'd just received had her stopped in her tracks.

"What's wrong?"

She put her phone away and glancing at him, kept walking. "I just got a text from my mother. She just not very technologically inclined. Apparently she just checked her phone messages and she had a call from the bank."

"Banks never call with good news."

She blew out a breath. "That's an understatement. It seems she'd been unknowingly dipping into the family fund. I guess we set it up that way back years ago."

Brandon wasn't sure what to say in response to that. It seemed a little like too much information. She'd gone from being almost completely closed off about anything personal to giving him financial information.

She gazed up him as they walked past the restaurant where they'd had dinner. "I really need that deal with Jafar."

And that, he thought, was why she was telling him this. "You're thinking about letting Jafar think we're engaged."

"Yeah." She bit her lip and made a face. "Like for real."

"How can we make it more real?"

"We'll have to think of something."

"Maybe you could sleep on it." He said the words with a straight face.

She laughed. "Yes. I'll sleep on it."

He took her hand and helped her into a carriage.

As they sat, each in their own thoughts, on the ride back the Grand Hotel, he realized he had much much more to think about than just his reaction to Annabelle back in the house.

He had to think about how he was going to pretend to be her fiancé when he didn't want to pretend.

He wanted it to be real.

CHAPTER 28

I could marry Jafar's son. Annabelle let that thought wash away as she showered. She did some of her best thinking in the shower. Thinking and sleeping. She didn't dare announce that little piece of information in a board meeting. She could just imagine the looks she would get. They'd start implementing plans to have her replaced.

She wouldn't be so lucky. She could probably make it with Jafar's deal, but she couldn't spend millions on a house if she let it drop.

It had been an eventful day. After a bumpy flight, she'd found that Jafar wanted her to marry his son in order to close a business deal. She'd discovered that the house her grandfather had wanted to buy years ago was now for sale. And now that she'd seen the inside of the house, she absolutely loved it.

She'd also discovered that she'd been able to talk to Brandon about her grandfather without going into a panic attack.

And... she'd discovered that she was really crushing on Brandon. A dangerous crush. A crush that could lead to an uncomfortable flight back.

A complicating factor was that she needed him to be her fake fiancé in order to close a deal that would allow her to buy a house she wanted and to protect her family's interests.

It's not fair to Brandon. Damn it. What was in it for him?

She couldn't just ask him to pretend to be her fiancé and give him nothing in return. It wasn't good business and wasn't a kind thing to do.

She stepped out of the shower and toweled off. She would have to ask him what he wanted in return. It was the only kind thing to do. She barely knew him, so there was no way she could second guess what he might want in return.

She climbed into bed and imagined what it would be like to be Brandon's fiancé. Being a fiancé usually involved kissing.

How could she have a fiancé she has never even kissed?

CHAPTER 29

*B*randon sat at the window of the Cupola Bar at the top of the Grand Hotel holding a crown on the rocks - his drink of choice when he was particularly troubled. He could see car lights traveling on the Mackinac Bridge.

He traveled a lot as a pilot working for Skye Travels and he visited a lot of pretty places. But this Mackinac Island had to be one of the most interesting. He would have to let his sister know that he now understood her fascination with the place.

Of course, it was just as possible that he was influenced by Annabelle's enthusiasm. She wanted to buy a house here. What twenty-three-year-old girl could walk into a house that went for at least a million dollars, maybe two, and decide on the spot that she was going to buy it?

He swirled the ice in his drink. The answer was no one, male or female, from his life experience. Sure, his boss Noah could, but that was to be expected. He wasn't twenty-three.

What was going on with him that he'd flipped for a girl who was at least as rich as his boss. He finished his drink and shoved it aside. One was enough. He needed to be alert tomorrow. Something would be up with Annabelle, though he had no idea what it would be. What would she come up with when she was *sleeping on it?*

He was pretty sure that she was going to need him to play the part of her fiancé. And he would do it. Of that he had no doubt. She wouldn't even have to ask.

Perhaps she'd cast some kind of island spell on him.

He turned and looked at the people sitting around, some alone like he was, but there were a lot of couples here. This was a place for couples. A romantic place. For people like his sister and her new husband.

Brandon considered himself well-traveled and worldly. But today had been outside his realm of experience. Annabelle was nothing if not intriguing.

Maybe that was it.

Or maybe he just needed to sleep on it.

CHAPTER 30

The next morning started before the sun was barely up. Annabelle got a text from Jafar inviting her to a breakfast meeting. Inviting was a nice way of saying he called a meeting.

As she ran a flat iron through her hair, she contemplated whether or not to ask Brandon to attend. If he were really her fiancé, as they'd claimed, would she have him go along? She'd never been engaged, but she was pretty sure the answer was yes. And they needed to walk into the meeting together. Jafar would expect them to be sharing a room.

By the time she was dressed and getting ready to go downstairs, she'd sent Brandon a text, but he didn't respond. Fortunately, she knew which room he was in. She pulled her handbag over her shoulders and went down the hall to his room.

Of course, he didn't answer. She knocked a second time and called his phone. When there was no answer, she called again and pressed her ear against his door. She thought she could hear a faint chiming ring tone.

The door opened and she fell right into his arms. Grabbing

her beneath her shoulders, Brandon help her regain her balance. "What are you doing?" He asked with a chuckle when she was safely back on her feet.

She crossed her arms. "You didn't answer your phone."

"It's six o'clock in the morning."

He was wearing sleep pants and a white tee-sheet. His hair was tousled and his eyes were still hooded with sleep. He hadn't shaved, of course, roughing his features with a hint of dark stubble. She swallowed hard. Unlike the clean-shaven pilot of yesterday, he was sporting a bad boy look. *Oh boy.* "I 'um..."

He crossed his arms and smiled smugly. "How did you find me?"

"I saw your key."

"Right." He took a step back and motioned for her to come inside.

"I shouldn't." She kept her feet planted where she stood.

"You need me, right?"

She flushed. "Jafar called a meeting."

"Okay. You can stand in the doorway while I take a shower."

She scowled at his back as he went toward the bathroom. "I can wait in the lobby."

He turned and grinned at her. "A fiancé wouldn't do that." Then closed the bathroom door.

"Fine." She huffed to herself and closed the door. He could have answered his phone. Either he slept like the dead or he chose to ignore her calls and messages.

She sat in the oversized chair and ran a hand along her black slacks. She wasn't sure if she was miffed at Brandon for not answering his phone or Jafar for summoning her to a meeting this early. Maybe a little of both.

Ten minutes later, he walked out of the bathroom, his hair wet, a towel wrapped around his waist. She put a hand over her eyes and checked her emails. Truly, the man should come with a hazard label.

"What is this meeting about so early in the morning?" He asked as he pulled on his pants.

"He didn't say."

The hangers rattled as he pulled a shirt from the little closet. "Have you decided what you're going to do?"

"Not a clue. My sleep process was interrupted.

He laughed. "I can empathize with you."

Now that he was dressed, she looked back up at him. Except for his wet hair, he was back to being the clean-shaven, professionally dressed pilot he'd been yesterday. Only now she knew what he looked like when he first woke up. And somehow that added a level of intimacy to their relationship. For her at least. He seemed unaffected.

"So are we the happy couple today?" He asked as he put his keys and money clip in his pockets. Again, more intimacy. She knew his morning routine, at least the quick version.

"Yes. At least until we find out what he's up to."

He held out his hand to help her up. Then hand in hand they left his room.

Annabelle's defenses slipped down another notch. Walking down the hall, hand in hand with Brandon felt perfectly natural.

CHAPTER 31

"I have another company willing to take the merger." Jafar announced.

Annabelle glanced from Jafar to his son. They were the only ones in the restaurant and other than the sound of dishes clinking together drifting from the kitchen, it was quiet. "You found someone to marry Kabir?" She couldn't resist asking. She found the whole situation so ridiculous it was hard to take it seriously.

Jafar shook his head. "No. The other investor has something else to offer."

Now he talking about investors. "What does this investor have to offer?"

"I can't tell you that. But the deal with you is better. So I'm giving you deadline."

Annabelle ran a finger along her glass of orange juice. "Deadline. I see." He was bluffing. She could spot a bluff from a mile away.

"Yes," Jafar continued. "We have wedding today."

Annabelle scoffed. "What wedding?"

"You choose. Kabir or him." He nodded toward Brandon.

"His name is Brandon."

Jafar ignored her. "I only merge with married woman."

Annabelle glared at Jafar, then shook her head. Brandon should have claimed to be her husband. Then they wouldn't be having this problem. It would be something else, no doubt.

No one spoke, the silence looming as the seconds passed. Then the server brought their food. Annabelle took a bite of melon, but it tasted like cardboard in her mouth. She swallowed and set down her fork. He'd already given her time to sleep on it, but she wasn't ready to make a decision. "I need time to think about it."

"What is there to think about?"

"We don't do marriage of convenience in our culture." She sighed. It was like beating her head against a wall. The man was not going to budge.

"I give you until eleven o'clock. I have chapel reserved"

Annabelle gaped at him. The man was insane. He was giving her less than four hours to make a decision about the rest of her life. And he knew it. He'd made it clear that he thought her engagement to Brandon was a sham. He was counting on Brandon backing out. It was one thing to pretend to be engaged to someone. It was another to stand up next to someone and actually marry them. "You can't do this."

Jafar smiled smugly. "I hold the cards as you say."

She narrowed her eyes. The man had put her in a situation she couldn't win.

"Annabelle." Brandon put a hand over hers. "Let's take some time and think about it."

"Of course," she said, regaining her composure.

CHAPTER 32

After breakfast that Annabelle barely touched, they grabbed a horse and carriage and rode downtown. They went to Starbuck's first, then wandered along the same trail they'd walked down the day before.

The sun was up now, the water glistening. And Brandon wasn't sure how to say to Annabelle. All he knew was that he wanted to fix it. To put the smile back on her face and for her to be happy again.

They reached the house that she wanted to buy and she sat on a rock on the other side of the trail.

Brandon walked across the trail and stared at the white house with the lighthouse wing. He turned and looked at the view across the lake.

Annabelle was looking down the trail back toward town, holding her coffee cup in both hands. He could see the creases between her brows. "Okay," he said, walking back toward her.

She watched him, but didn't respond.

"So let's look at what you want. Since you're too emotionally involved, maybe I can help. You have two objectives, right? You want to buy this house and you want to take care of your mother." He waited until she nodded to continue.

"So you have to do whatever it takes to get there."

"You make it sound so simple."

"Will signing this deal with Jafar get you those two things?"

"As far as I can tell, yes."

"Then all you have to do is sign with him and it's yours." He waved a hand toward the house.

She shook her head and looked away. "I'm not marrying that man."

"You don't have to. All he wants to see is a wedding."

"Don't be ridiculous."

There was only one way this was going to work.

She would have to marry Brandon.

Unfortunately, she didn't seem to see that as a viable option.

CHAPTER 33

This had been a bad idea. It was hard to concentrate with the house behind her and Brandon pacing in front of her. She wanted the house and well… she was crushing on Brandon.

But there was no way she would ask Brandon to go through with a sham marriage and there wasn't a chance in hell that she was going to marry Kabir. Not for any amount of money.

He stopped and stood directly in front of her. She looked up at him. "There's only one way to fix this."

She shook her head and looked away again.

"Annabelle." He put a finger under her chin and gently urged her to look up at him. "You have to marry me."

She scoffed. "You're insane."

"I'm trying not to be insulted."

"What do you mean?"

"Never mind." He turned and looked away.

"Why?" She asked. "Why would you marry me? I don't understand what's in it for you."

Her idea of offering a kiss in return for marrying her seemed ludicrous in the light of day.

"I don't want anything." He sounded tired.

"I'm sorry for dragging you into this."

He looked back at her. "You seem to have forgotten that I got myself into it. I don't recall you asking for anything."

"You were just being kind."

He laughed. "Trust me. I don't go around being kind to just anyone."

She would have laughed under any other circumstances. Instead she just blinked back the tears that she would not allow to be seen.

CHAPTER 34

*H*e could see the pain in her eyes. Pain that he wanted so badly to take away. But if marrying him added to her distress, he truly was at a loss as to how to help her. "I'm saying that we can go through with his wedding, you can sign the merger, and everyone can go home happy. You can buy this house and take care of your mother."

She sighed. "I don't know how wise it is to sign a contract with a man like that."

"I don't know anything about the merger itself. Once you sign, do you have to continue to interact with him?"

"No. It's more like selling to him, really."

"Then what's the worst that could happen?"

"He wins."

He smiled to himself at the little pout that formed on her lips when she said those words out loud. And then he realized that if it took pretending to marry her in order to kiss her, marry her he would.

The only problem was he had to convince her to agree to marry him.

CHAPTER 35

$\mathcal{A}$nnabelle bit her lip. She needed to think. There was too much going on. Too many emotions. Emotions and business don't mix. She could have managed the thing with her mother. There were other options. Except now there was this house. This house that her grandfather had planned to buy someday.

She walked to the edge of the lawn and looked at the lighthouse wing, with so many windows, it was almost made out of glass. She imagined sitting on the little swing and watching the sunset. Watching people walk and bicycle past on the trail. She could fly to Dallas when she needed to. It didn't take long. All she had to do was send a message to Noah and a plane would be here for her within three hours.

She wasn't sure about the winters. But having months to read by the fireplace sounded like absolute bliss. She could get a cat.

That did it. She turned back to Brandon. "Let's get some breakfast and work out a deal." She checked her watch. She needed to call her attorney. He wasn't at work yet, but she needed a prenup and she needed it quick.

As they walked back down the trail, she phoned her attorney. He could have a prenup document ready to sign electronically in less than an hour. She put Brandon on the phone for his address and other pertinent information.

They went to a little restaurant and ordered a hearty breakfast of eggs, bacon, and toast.

"Want to fill me in on the details?" Brandon asked as they ate.

"Like you said, it's simple. We sign the prenup, do the deal, then we just don't file the paperwork so it's like it never happened."

"What if Jafar insists we file the paperwork?"

"He won't. I'm going to insist he sign the papers before we go through with it." She swallowed a bite of toast. "Or." She shrugged. "Worst case scenario we file for an annulment."

"Are you sure there's nothing in his contract about the length of a marriage or anything like that?"

"I have the document on my iPad. My attorney has read it, I've read it. No where in there does it say anything about marriage. He just wants me to marry his son so he can be legal and he's calling my bluff."

"It doesn't make any sense."

"None." She smiled and bit into a bite of bacon. Annabelle hadn't eaten bacon since she was twelve. But she was about to buy a multi-million-dollar house on Mackinac Island. That called for a little indulgence.

And she was about to *marry* a handsome man. A man who she liked. A lot.

CHAPTER 36

*E*verything moved quickly over the next two hours. When the downtown shops opened at ten o'clock they had split up. Annabelle went in search of a dress while Brandon found a place where he could rent a tux off the rack. While he waited for her, he wandered into the shop next door and was drawn to their jewelry counter.

He was sure he wasn't supposed to buy her a ring, but when he saw it, he knew it was perfect. He pulled out his credit card and walked out with a smile on his face.

When they got back to the hotel, Jafar was waiting for them. Annabelle and Brandon dashed upstairs to their respective rooms to get dressed.

As he showered, Brandon found his mind going in a hundred different directions, but he quickly gave up on trying to figure out Annabelle's sudden change of heart. He'd been so thrown off balance, he hadn't even asked her what had tipped her decision.

In truth, he thought, as he toweled off and got dressed, he didn't need to know. All he knew was that he was about to marry Annabelle Lawson, one of the most beautiful and intriguing girls he'd ever spent time with.

Besides, he thought as he buttoned the vest of his black three-piece suit, he wasn't one to judge. He'd been struck with cupid's arrow standing there in the very house that Annabelle was planning to buy.

CHAPTER 37

$\mathcal{A}$nnabelle had found a white dress in one of the downtown shops. It was more flowing than she usually wore – a full skirt that stopped just below her knees and a sweetheart neckline. It was not only white, but it was a perfect fit.

Her fingers trembled as she zipped up the back of the dress. She wore her lace-up boots because they were the only shoes she'd brought and besides she thought they looked kinda cute. She dropped one of her earring backs and spent five minutes tracking it down. How did they always disappear so easily?

Finally, with her make-up touched up, she stood in front of the mirror and took a deep breath.

My wedding day.

It wasn't what she'd plan or what she'd expected it to be, but here it was. Real or not, it certainly felt real. And Brandon was someone she could see herself marrying.

She picked up her hairbrush and brushed her hair again. Took a little bottle of perfume she rarely wore, sprayed it into the air and walked through it.

She checked her phone. It was time for Brandon. Almost by magic, he knocked on her door.

They stood in the open doorway, staring at each other.

"You're beautiful." He whispered.

She smiled. "You look handsome."

"We should take a picture," he said, pulling his phone out of his pocket.

They posed for a selfie, both grinning like teens on a first date. "Send it to me," she said.

"We should go."

She grabbed her messenger bag, looped it over her shoulder, and followed him out the door.

He sent her the picture as they walked down the hall, down the stairs, and hurried to the little wedding chapel. "Are you sure you know where it is?" She asked as they raced down the long foyer.

"I'm positive." He answered just as they reached the chapel door.

Someone put a bouquet of white roses in her hand as they entered the room. She saw Jafar and Kabir sitting along with a couple of people she'd never seen before.

Annabelle held onto Brandon's arm as they walked toward the priest.

The priest.

She froze and her feet refused to move forward.

"What's wrong?" Brandon asked in her ear.

His breath sent tingles down her spine. This was just a faux wedding to get a foreign investor off her back so they could sign a business deal and move forward.

So she could buy the house she and her grandfather had talked about buying all those years ago before he'd gotten sick and passed away.

It was a faux wedding.

They'd signed all the legal paperwork to make sure it was a

marriage in name only. They even had an annulment signed just in case Jafar insisted they file the marriage certificate making it binding.

There was just one snag.

The priest standing before them was real.

CHAPTER 38

"Brandon." She put both her hands on his arm and whispered so only he could hear. "There's a priest."

"Of course. It's customary."

"I think he's real."

Brandon was focused on calming his own jitters. He'd expected Annabelle to back out by now. So she'd made it further than he'd expected.

She was focused on the priest. "So?

"Brandon…"

"It's okay. Come on. Let's just get this over with so we can go make an offer on your house."

That seemed to spur her forward. Once they stood in front of the priest and he began to recite the traditional wedding vows, the thing Annabelle had been trying to tell him sank in.

He looked over at her, her attention focused on every word spoken by the priest. Her cheeks had a becoming flush. His heart was racing. Annabelle Lawson was standing at the alter next to him.

He'd only known her a short time, but in that short time, he'd gotten to know her, and he not only was attracted to her, he liked her. He liked everything about her. The way she smiled at him. He even found her beautiful when she was annoyed with him.

"Do you Brandon Barrett take this woman, Annabelle Lawson to love honor and cherish for the rest of your life?"

"I…" And in that moment, he understood what she'd been trying to tell him. Everything about this wedding was a sham.

Except the priest.

The priest was real.

If the priest was real, this marriage was real in the eyes of God.

CHAPTER 39

The little chapel was quiet. So quiet she could hear her own breath. The priest standing before them didn't have reason to care if this was a faux marriage or a real marriage. To him, it was obviously a real marriage.

Annabelle was mesmerized by the priest – his soothing voice. The words, some familiar, some not. She wasn't Catholic, but she'd been to the Catholic church on occasion. Even a Catholic wedding once with a college friend.

She heard the priest ask Brandon if he would love, honor, and cherish her for the rest of her life. *It's not real. It's not real.*

She waited for what must have been mere seconds, but seemed like an eternity for him to answer. He said the word *I* then stopped.

She turned and saw that he was staring at her, his eyes moist. He took both her hands in his and gazing into her eyes, said. "I Brandon Barrett take you Annabelle Lawson to love, honor, and cherish for the rest of my life."

The priest, seemingly unaffected, started talking again. He was asking Annabelle the same question he'd asked Brandon.

She was spell-bound by his soft gaze, his lips turned up at the corners. "Yes," she whispered.

After that, the priest's words blurred into the background. The blood was pounding in her ears. In this moment, all the paperwork they had signed meant nothing.

"Do you have a ring?" The priest asked.

They didn't have rings. Who would think to buy a ring for a fake marriage?

Then Brandon took her hand and slipped a ring on her finger. She gasped. It was a beautiful rose gold band with a sparkly diamond in the middle. The perfect blend of engagement ring and wedding band.

Brandon had not just gotten her a ring, he gotten her the most perfect ring.

The priest paused again. Brandon released her hands and dipped his head close. Before she had time to think, his lips were pressed against hers.

"I now pronounce you husband and wife."

CHAPTER 40

*B*randon had died and gone to heaven. His lips pressed against Annabelle's set every nerve in his body on fire.

He pulled back enough to gaze into her eyes. Her expression was one of wonder. Perhaps this was surreal to her, too.

Following the priest's instructions, he took her hand and they turned to face the small audience that included a couple of hotel staff members.

He smiled smugly at Jafar and Kabir. They watched with a cool dispassion. It was time for them to sign the paperwork for the merger.

"You have your iPad?" It wasn't the most romantic first sentence for a husband to say to his wife. But in this case, it might just be the most appropriate.

"Yes." She opened her messenger bag and pulled out her iPad. With just a few clicks, she had the merger document pulled up.

Her gaze steady now, she walked to a little table and

motioned for Jafar to join her. She pulled her Apple pencil out and held it out to him.

For just a moment, Brandon thought he was going to refuse to sign.

But after he hesitated just long enough to make his point, he signed the document. Annabelle signed after him. Then shot the document off to her attorney.

She turned back to Brandon. It was time to sign the marriage certificate.

CHAPTER 41

$\mathcal{I}$n this moment, she was married to Brandon Barrett.

But then as she watched Jafar sign the merger document, she was jarred back to reality. This was the purpose of the marriage. Now she could get on with her life.

Now she could buy the house here on the island and take another step forward toward her dream of starting a publishing company.

Her mother would be financially taken care of, so that would be one less thing she would have to worry about.

Everything was falling into place.

Brandon stood next to her as they signed their marriage certificate. Her hands trembled so that she barely recognized her own signature. It felt so real.

And she recognized that she wanted it to be real. She wanted to marry Brandon for real. Not with paperwork stating that it was for business only.

But for love.

His kiss had been everything she'd imagined. Her only regret was that it would be the only kiss they would share. She wanted more.

But right now, they had to continue the charade.

A member of the hotel staff brought out champagne goblets filled with sparkling wine.

Jafar inched close as they signed the marriage certificate, then slipped out, taking Kabir with him.

After a few words of congratulations and well wishes, the priest and hotel staff members left them alone.

"What do we do now?" Annabelle mused quietly.

Brandon took her hands in hands, pressed his lips lightly against the backs of her fingers. "For now," he said. "we're husband and wife."

Annabelle's cheeks heated as she imagined all sorts of things under his intense gaze. "I suppose we are."

"Want to go downtown and get some lunch?"

It was such an ordinary question. Suddenly it seemed like nothing had changed. Feeling a little disoriented, she turned her phone off vibrate and checked her messages. "Sure," She said as she read her texts. She sent off a quick response. "Let's go."

While they walked to the front door, she sent some texts back and forth.

They stood in the cool air with the soft sunlight and waited for a carriage. Annabelle checked the time. It looked like they had just enough time.

"Everything okay?" Brandon asked.

"Oh." She smiled at him, realizing she'd been lost in thought. "My attorney will be here at two o'clock."

CHAPTER 42

"Your attorney?" Brandon echoed. "Here?" She nodded. "On the island?"

"Yeah. He's landing at the airport."

Brandon helped his new wife into the horse drawn carriage and sat down beside her. He attempted to wrap his brain around this new information. "Your attorney from Dallas?"

She nodded.

"Why?"

"To make sure all the paperwork is in order." At his questioning expression, she continued. "The house. The merger. The marriage."

It was a good thing he was sitting down. The ground dropped out from under him in one fell swoop.

He looked away, watched as they passed the little cottages on the way to town. Passed a group of tourists walking toward the hotel. A couple taking pictures of each other.

People doing normal things.

He was sitting next to a woman who bought a multi-million-dollar house on an island across the country from where she lived and worked. Who had an attorney flown in just to make sure all the paperwork was in order. Paperwork to buy a house and complete a business merger that allowed her to buy said house.

And then on top of that, she married the most convenient guy around to make sure all this fell into place and keep the pressure off of her to marry a man from India who used marriage as a bargaining chip.

Sure, Brandon was a successful pilot which carried a certain amount of prestige with it, but this, this world Annabelle was living and saw as perfectly ordinary, was completely outside his realm of reality.

Normal people didn't do that. Today his mother would be at work at her job where someone else set her schedule and she hoped to earn enough money to save up for a trip to Disneyland. She'd never been there so she and a coworker were making plans to go. Next year. Maybe. If they could save up enough money and get the time off they would go.

Brandon's mother had helped him through college. She'd helped him pay the price to get where he was. But he still owed money on student loans. He lived in a two-bedroom condo with a view of the pool. It was the nicest place he'd ever lived. He hoped to *someday* have enough money to buy a condo or maybe a house in the suburbs.

He looked over at Annabelle, busy on her phone again. Little diamond earring sparkled at her ears and on her neck. Nothing gaudy. In fact, someone had to be standing directly in front of her to even see them. He then looked at the little ring he'd placed on her finger. He'd thought it was a nice cross between and engagement ring and wedding band. It had a little faux diamond set in the middle of a rose gold band. The stone was a cubic zirconia as wide as the band.

The ring was completely out of place on her. He'd paid two hundred dollars for it. It was a faux wedding after all. A faux ring for a faux wedding.

But even if it had been a real wedding, it would have been impossible for him to even come close to being able to walk into Tiffany's and buy her the type of ring she would be accustomed to. That would never happen.

These three days were nothing more than a fantasy. An aberration in Brandon's life that would never happen again. Annabelle was like a fairy princess. Someone he could stand near, but never touch. He could never really be a part of her world.

He'd allowed himself, just for a moment in time, to imagine that the wedding had been real and even if the wedding wasn't real, that the relationship blossoming between them was real. It wasn't real. Even if they had an attraction, they could never be in a real relationship. She was too outside his league.

"Want to go to the tavern again for lunch?" She asked they rode down main street.

"Sure."

CHAPTER 43

nnabelle felt sick. Minutes later they were seated at a table in the little restaurant.

Brandon wouldn't even look at her.

The server brought them water.

There was a lump in her throat. Ever since she'd told him that her attorney was flying in, he he'd barely said two words and he hadn't looked at her at all.

"Brandon? What's wrong?"

"There's nothing wrong," he said.

So now that the wedding was over, he was ready to go on his way.

"Thank you," she said.

He looked at her then and she saw something in his eyes she couldn't quite understand. It looked like a cross between sadness and distance. "For what?"

She swallowed, but the pain in her heart was nearly unbearable. "Thank you for marrying me." She felt the tears falling from her eyes. She couldn't stop them. "I have to-"

She stood up and rushed blindly to the restroom. She closed

the door and let the pain wash over her and the sobs consume her. She couldn't stop it if she'd tried.

Five minutes later, she rinsed her face. So much for make-up. She dried her face and steadied herself.

It wasn't his fault she'd gone and fallen for him. That hadn't been part of the deal.

It was time to go back out there and set Brandon free.

CHAPTER 44

Brandon kicked himself. He couldn't have handled this more badly if he'd purposely set out to hurt her.

He was only trying to get out of her way so she could be happy. Unfortunately, his own pain had been so overwhelming, he hadn't considered her feelings.

By the time he'd convinced himself to go after her, she was headed back to their table. He could tell she'd been crying. Her make-up was washed off and her face was flushed.

He hated himself for being the one to do that to her.

He wanted to be the man who always made her happy. But he didn't deserve her. She belonged in another world. A world he would never belong to.

Since he couldn't get to her level, he wasn't going to bring here down to his.

She sat at the table and tried to smile. "I know that you only did this out of the kindness of your heart," she said.

"I did it because I wanted to."

"But you didn't have to and for that I'm eternally grateful. I just want you to know that I don't have any expectations for you. I won't file the certificate. I'll keep it in case there's ever a problem, but I won't file it. So, legally, we were never married."

"I'm not sure it works like that." He wanted to tell her that he felt married to her. That the ceremony had been real to him. But she obviously didn't want to hear that. Even now, she was ready to be rid of him. "Look," he said. "I'm gonna head out. I'll be there in the morning to fly you back as planned. I don't know where the hell Beau is, but he'll show up."

"Brandon…"

"I'll be out of your way now. I hope it all goes well with the house."

He slid his chair back and stood up.

Then he did one of the hardest things he'd ever done.

He walked away from Annabelle Lawson. The girl who had his heart.

CHAPTER 45

Ten days later

Brandon taxied down the runway at Will Rogers World Airport in Oklahoma City. He'd made a perfectly smooth landing. But then the airport had been a breeze to navigate. Nothing like Mackinac Island. It had only been ten days, but already, the island was becoming nothing more than a memory.

His flight today was a quick one – out and back. He was flying Hermon Hampton up to pick up his wife who'd been visiting with family.

Brandon secured the plane. This was his favorite kind of trip. One pilot. One passenger. Well, two on the way back. He could be home in time for dinner.

Hermon was in his late forties, maybe early fifties. He'd been content to read his Kindle, leaving Brandon alone with own thoughts for the short flight.

"She's running late." Hermon announced when he turned on his phone.

"Okay." Such was the nature of the business. "How much?"

Herman checked his watch. "About three hours."

They'd be exiting the plane then.

"Sorry about that." Herman unhooked his safety harness. "Can I buy you lunch?"

"Nope." Brandon grinned. "But Skye Travels will buy yours."

"If it suits you, it suits me."

Brandon called for a car and thirty minutes later, they were seated at a Mexican restaurant. Herman ordered a margarita, but Brandon drank water.

"Still on the job."

Herman sipped his drink. "You don't know what you're missing."

"I can imagine. How long has your wife been up here?"

"Two weeks. Her sister was in an accident and Milly came up to stay with her. It seems like a life-time since I've seen her."

"Two weeks can seem like a long time." Brandon thought about how it had been almost two weeks since he'd seen Annabelle. It felt like an eternity.

"Yeah. I'm not used to staying in that big ole house by myself."

"How long have you been married?" The server brought chips and salsa. Herman jumped right in."

"Thirty-two years."

"Wow."

"This is the longest we've been apart."

"You had to stay back and work?"

"Work? Nah. I haven't had to work in years. I stayed home to take care of the dogs. We had puppies three weeks ago and I couldn't go off and leave them. They would've forgotten who I am by now."

Brandon chuckled. He certainly met some interesting people in this line of work.

"Millie. She wanted me to hire a sitter. But I'm old fashioned I guess."

"Seems reasonable to me." Brandon said absently as he ate chips and salsa.

"Are you married?"

"No." He ignored the flash of emotion that crashed over him like a bolt of lightning.

"Ah." Hermon waved his hand. "When I was your age, I didn't care about settling down." He sat back. "Meeting Millie saved me."

"What do you mean?"

"I was a bit down on my luck. I was a professional golfer, but I couldn't quite break in the big time." He stared into space. "I met Millie outside a country club. Ah. She was everything I could never be."

Brandon leaned forward wanting to know more. "What do you mean?"

"She was the daughter of a wealthy man. In fact, her father practically owned the country club of the little town we were in. He owned the bank and a lot of other things in the town. I don't know. It was a small little town.

"It was love at first sight. When I saw her, I knew I'd do anything for her."

Brandon held his breath. "It didn't bother you that she was rich?"

"Oh sure." Brandon chuckled. "At first it did, but it didn't matter. I didn't even know it for the first two months. I thought she worked at the country club. She let me believe it. We'd meet in town. Or at my place. It took all the money I had to rent a little cabin on the outside of town. My father was a postman. I remember one year we didn't even get Christmas gifts. There wasn't enough money. Oh, but you don't want to hear this. I'm boring you."

"No. No. Please go on."

"Oh. Okay. She was afraid it would bother me. That's why

she didn't tell me. We talked about how we'd run away and find work somewhere. It was very romantic."

"How did you find out?"

"When I asked her to marry me, she said no." The server brought their food then and interrupted his story.

"And?" As soon as the server left, Brandon urged him to continue. He wanted – needed to know what happened next.

"Ah. Yes. She told me I had to meet her family first. And then if I still wanted to marry her I could ask her again."

"So all that time you didn't know who she was?"

"Oh. I knew who she was. She was beautiful and kind and funny and set my heart aflutter every time I saw her. The rest didn't matter."

"So you met them?"

"Oh yeah. They were nice people. A little eccentric, but then who isn't."

"So you asked her again?"

"Nah. I asked her father first. He said he wanted to get to know me first. So I went to play golf with him. Everyday for a week." Herman chuckled. "I beat him every time. I think he was rather impressed. But I'd played professionally, so in all truthfulness it wasn't really fair. At the end of that week, he gave me permission to marry his daughter. I was so happy, I asked her right there. I got down on my knees right there in front of her mother and father and brother. It was right after Sunday dinner, so they were all there. Playing croquet on the lawn of all things."

"So it never bothered you?"

"Nah. It didn't change who we were. In fact, I helped her with some business things and she helped me. She started me up in my own business." He chuckled. "I might even have more money than she does. We stopped counting."

Brandon absorbed all this. His story seemed so unlikely. "What kind of business do you have?"

Herman's cell phone rang interrupting them. He got up and went to stand just outside the door of the restaurant. Brandon saw him pacing and forth as he talked.

Brandon pushed his plate aside and paid the server.

He went up front and sat on a bench next to the door while he waited for Herman to finish his phone call. While he waited, he flipped through the photos on his phone and came to the picture of the two them moments before they went downstairs to the chapel to get married. They looked so happy. Her face was glowing. And he remembered well that his own smile had been genuine.

He looked at Herman, a man who had come from nothing. Just like Brandon. And looking at him now, no one would ever know that he came from a poor background – even more so than Brandon.

He zoomed in on Annabelle's face and his heart broke. He'd assumed too much. He'd made her decision for her. He'd had no right to do that.

He'd made a mess.

CHAPTER 46

Annabelle looked out the window one last time. From here she had a clear view of the better part of the Dallas skyline. It had been a good office. But now she didn't need it anymore. The merger was complete and the company would run itself now. With the help of a company based out of India. New management. She had a place on the board of directors if she wanted it. That was a decision for later.

She had three crates of personal items packed and ready to go.

She put her handbag over her shoulder and called for her car. While she waited, she turned the little wedding ring Brandon had given her. It was a little big, so she wore it on her left index finger. It was the only jewelry she wore other than her earrings and the necklace her grandfather had given her. She wore jewelry given to her by both of the men she carried in her heart.

It had been two weeks since her wedding to Brandon. The unfiled marriage certificate was at home, in a little wall safe behind a faux Monet print. She found it ironic to put a certificate for a faux wedding behind a faux painting.

It may have been for convenience only, but in her heart, it had been real. The flight from Mackinac to Dallas hadn't been as bad as she'd expected, but that was only because her interactions were only with Beau Armstrong. He hadn't said where he'd spent the last three days and she hadn't asked. She hadn't wanted to talk about what she had done either.

The front desk buzzed her phone informing her that her car was ready.

She left her old office behind and turned her thoughts toward the future.

She went through the lobby and out the front door. Her BMW sedan was parked to the side instead of being pulled up front like it usually was.

She looked around for the valet, but she didn't see anyone. Hopefully he'd left her key fob in the car.

There was a limo out front. He'd probably parked it out of the way of the limo. The driver was standing out in front of it, leaning against the side of the limo. He wore dark shades and a driver's cap.

As she approached, he straightened. Took a step forward.

She froze. He looked... familiar.

She shook her head. It was the sunlight. Even in October, the Dallas sun could be deadly. She was hallucinating. She started walking again.

When she was four feet from him, he stepped in front of her, and lowered his sunshades.

She stopped, her feet glued to the sidewalk.

Brandon stood in front of her, grinning like a loon. "Can I offer you transportation?"

She crossed her arms. "I have a car."

"But do you have a driver?"

She scowled. "I can drive."

He laughed. "All right then." He tipped his hat and turned around as though to leave.

"Wait."

He turned back. Looked at her questioningly.

"What are you doing here?"

"I came to offer you a ride."

"But... I... Why?"

He held out his hand. "I'd rather show you."

She was so very confused. She rubbed her thumb against the rose gold ring on her finger. The man she'd fallen in love with was standing before her. She had to see whatever it was he wanted. She put her hand in his.

He helped her into the back seat of the limo, closed the door and went around to the driver's seat.

"Why didn't you get a driver?"

"You'll see." He bucked his seat belt. "There's champagne back there if you want it."

She turned her gaze to the back seat. There was an ice bucket with uncorked bottle of champagne. And two glasses. She shrugged and filled one of them.

She took a sip as he pulled out into traffic.

"Where are we going?"

He turned on some music. She recognized Bach. "Just sit back, relax, and let me surprise you."

"He's gone insane." She muttered. But she leaned back, closed her eyes, and took some deep breaths.

About thirty minutes later, he stopped the car and turned off the motor. She couldn't tell where they were, but when he opened her door, she recognized the smell of jet fuel. They were at the airport?

She stepped out of the car and he took off his shades and his hat laying them on the seat behind her.

They were parked at the edge of the airport. An airplane took off overhead, and they waited until it had passed.

Then Brandon was on his knees in front of her with both her hands in his.

CHAPTER 47

$\mathcal{B}$randon's heart was pounding so fast he could barely think.

He was putting himself out on a limb. Way out on a limb. "Annabelle Lawson."

She was looking at him sideways. If he hadn't been so nervous, he would have laughed.

"I have something to tell you.

"Okay."

"I know I can't offer you the things you're used to. I can't buy you expensive jewelry or clothes or... houses."

She bit her lip. "I don't care about that. I can buy whatever I need."

"I don't have much to offer you financially." He needed to say it out loud. "But-" He swept a hand back toward the airplanes, I can offer you the world."

"What do you mean?"

"I love you Annabelle and I want to spend the rest of my life with you. I can't give you things, but I can fly you anywhere you want to go."

She didn't say anything.

"Annabelle, will you marry me?"

"Yes." She didn't hesitate.

This was not what he had expected. "Don't you want to sleep on it?"

She laughed. "Nope. This is one decision I don't have to sleep on. I'm sure."

He stood up and hugging her, pulled her off her feet to twirl in a circle. Then he set her on her feet. "You really mean it?"

"Brandon," she said. "We're already married."

He hugged her again. She'd said the exact thing that he'd been thinking for two weeks. They were already married.

CHAPTER 48

$\mathcal{A}$nnabelle didn't know how Brandon had found her. Or he'd worked his way around to proposing, but she did know that there was nothing she wanted more than to be married to him.

The morning they had gotten married had been one of the happiest times of her adult life. Even knowing it wasn't real, she'd been happy.

And, she realized, that morning, that it was real. They'd been married by a priest in the eyes of God.

It didn't get much more real than that.

"We have to catch our flight," he said. "But there's just one thing."

"What is it?"

"Do you still have our marriage license?"

"Of course. It's at my house."

"Great. Let's run grab it and you pack a bag."

"Where are we going?"

"Michigan. We have to file a certificate to make our marriage legal. Then we have a reservation at the Grand Hotel."

Two hours later, they boarded a little Cessna airplane.

As she stepped into the cabin, Samuel stood there smiling at her.

"Samuel?" She hugged him. Then stepped back into Brandon's arms. "I thought..." He wrapped his arms around her and kissed her cheek.

"Brandon wanted you to be flown by the best pilot on your honeymoon. He wanted to make sure you had a smooth landing this time."

EPILOGUE

*I*t was cold outside. So cold Lake Huron was frozen and snow was banked on the windows of the lighthouse wing of the house.

But inside was warm. Annabelle sat on the couch, her feet in Brandon's lap, a stack of novel submissions on the floor beside her. She liked the printed copies so she could take notes on them.

Brandon worked on his laptop, revising her website.

Life was good.

Three two-month old kittens ran rough and tumble around the room, the mother cat stretched in front of the fireplace.

"We should really give them names," Annabelle said picking up the white kitten and putting it on the couch. "We can't keep calling this one white kitten. And the other gray kitten and black kitten."

"We'll think of something. After we figure out their personalities."

"I'm not sure we're good parents."

"We're perfect parents." He picked up the white kitten in one hand and it mewled. They laughed.

"I think you have to give a baby a name before you take it from the hospital."

"Aw. But these are babies." He put the kitten in his lap on its back and it attacked his hand with all four little feet.

"Maybe we should practice."

"We can give them names if you want to."

She smiled to herself. "I think we should start looking at baby names now. Our track record for picking names isn't so good."

"We'll think of something for these babies."

"Not these babies."

Brandon turned and looked at her, his eyes wide. Annabelle smiled sweetly. "A baby?"

She nodded.

He grabbed her up, papers flying everywhere and twirled her around the room.

She giggled.

He set her on her feet and nuzzled her ear. "I love you so so much."

"I love you, too."

Annabelle's heart was filled with happiness. She had the house she'd always dreamed of. And a fairy tale romance with her very own handsome pilot.

Want to read more second chance romance? How about a bonus short story?

<u>GET MY BONUS SHORT STORY</u>
https://BookHip.com/DXPMJDT

Keep reading for a preview of *Just Maybe...* the next sweet wholesome story in the *Worthington Family Collection...*

KATHRYN KALEIGH
Just
Maybe
FOR THE LOVE OF THE FLIGHT

CHAPTER 1

Tara Montgomery leaned over and shoved a stack of heavy cardboard boxes two feet to the right and studied the corroded fuse box in the musty smelling storage room. She was alone in the back of Aunt Avery's shop *Falling Snow*. She had on J Crew jeans, a light charcoal tank that hugged her bottom under a hip length black cardigan, and little lace up ankle boots. She shivered and rubbed her hands over her arms.

October in Texas was still warm, and could even be hot, but here on Mackinac Island the temperature was already down to the lower forties. She was told that it was usually much warmer this time of year. It was just her luck to be here during a cold spell. And it was looking like she was going to be here through the winter. It wouldn't be her first choice, but family came first. And her father's sister had been there for them when Tara's sister had gotten sick. Aunt Avery's husband had been alive then, so her leaving the shop here on the island hadn't been a disaster. That had been eight years ago though and things had changed.

Right about now Tara's sorority sisters would be sitting in class at Louisiana Tech getting ready for lunch at Roma Italian Bistro. Tara was stuck here in Michigan running a store. Not only had she not even visited here since she was a child, but she knew absolutely nothing about running a store. She was majoring in English, so she kept her head in a book most of the time.

She would miss the social events this Fall, but she really didn't mind. She'd gotten her fill of all that last year. Now in her second year of college, she stayed in the sorority mostly for her resume. The one positive coming out of this was that she had lots of time to read the books required for her classes which had all been moved online. That was another perk of being in the sorority. The administration worked closely with her to keep her enrolled while she was away from campus.

Using the pad of one finger, careful not to nick her perfectly painted rose-colored nails, she opened the little rusty door. It creaked like a door in an old horror movie and she glanced over her shoulder. Katness, her aunt's white Himalayan cat sat on his haunches, watching her with his bright blue eyes. He blinked as though to say *go ahead.* She shrugged and turned back to the fuse box.

There were ten round fuses, with handwritten labels next to the them. Her Aunt Avery had said it was old, but it was *really* old. The glass on the fuses had yellowed with age and the labels were peeling, the writing faded. She lightly touched the top right glass fuse labeled *shop.* Taking a deep breath, she grasped it and twisted it to the left. At first it didn't move. She wiped her hand on her jeans and tried again, giving it all her strength. It turned, grinding like sand against metal, little dust particles falling to the floor. A few more turns and it was loose in her hand. Heaving a sigh of relief, she set it aside on one of the boxes.

She took the new fuse out of her sweater pocket and stuck it into the groove, lining the threads just right and twisting it in place. Just as it tightened, it popped. She yelped and jumped back.

Now this one was blown. And it was their last good fuse.

The shop had some light filtering in from the windows along the front, but without overhead lights, it was almost impossible to see the details on the little snow globes. Not exactly a good shopping experience.

Now what?

She pulled her iPhone out of her back pocket and dialed her aunt's phone. She heard it ringing in her aunt's room upstairs. "The new fuse burned out."

"I don't have anymore fuses." Aunt Avery told her.

"What do we do?"

"Put a penny in it."

Tara studied the round fuses. *A penny?* She didn't carry cash, much less a penny. Never had. Having grown up in Dallas, Texas, she always had a credit card. No one in her group of friends carried cash. "Put a penny where?"

"Take the fuse out and put a penny in its place."

"Ok." What else could she say? Her aunt had a broken leg and wouldn't be coming downstairs for weeks. Maybe months. She was sixty-four, so she had to be extra cautious.

She hung up the phone and with Katness at her heels, went back out into the shop – the dark shop with no lights.

Two elderly women stepped just inside the front door. The little bell over the door tinkled cheerily. "Are you open?"

"Yeah. Just a problem with the power."

"Oh." They looked at each other. "We'll come back by." They slipped out the door, leaving Tara staring helplessly after them. A fine job she was doing. Her aunt had summoned her up to Mackinac Island to save the shop and Tara could barely get anyone in the door.

. . .

CHAPTER 2

Beau Erickson hooked his finger into the collar of his black suit jacket and tossed it over his shoulder. The soft breeze coming off of Lake Huron brought welcomed cool air to the skin beneath his white cotton button-down shirt.

Shortly after landing at Mackinac Island airport, their single passenger, Annabelle Lawson had taken a horse drawn carriage and gone ahead to the hotel while he and his copilot Brandon secured the twin engine Lear jet. Then he and Brandon had ridden in their own horse drawn taxi to the Grand Hotel where they had reservations.

Beau had been a lot of places, but he hadn't even known that a place like this existed. The red and gold maple trees splashed color along the paved path as they road into town. The clip clop of the horse's hooves on the pavement was soothing. Beau had relaxed against the wooden seat of the wagon and breathed the crisp clean air.

After asking the carriage driver to wait, he'd checked in, had his luggage sent to the room, and rode downtown. The driver had dropped him off near the dock. About a hundred people got off the ferry and made their way ashore.

No cars on Mackinac Island. The downtown streets were crowded with horse drawn taxis, bicycles, and people on foot. After passing the dock on his left, the street was lined with two rows of quaint two story buildings. The bottom story was covered with awnings over the sidewalk. The upper stories were mostly old-fashioned facades. Wrought iron signs advertised everything from fudge shops to antique stores to a Starbucks store.

Further down, he saw a white four story building with balconies on each floor – a charming inn. The lamp posts were decorated with little American flags. Beau felt a surge of pride.

He'd done his four years in the Air Force after being in ROTC while getting his degree in aviation.

As he wandered the street, watching the tourists, he relaxed. Three days. He had three days of freedom to enjoy the island.

Flying for Skye Travels was by far the best possible job. He'd only been working for Noah Worthington for six months, but already he was hooked. Beau didn't have a lot of experience flying in the private sector. It took different mindset than flying in the military. But Noah had taken a chance on him.

After stopping at a little restaurant for a hamburger and fries, he wandered into a couple of shops. He walked through a souvenir shop and a tee-shirt shop, then stepped back outside stood on the sidewalk watching the tourists wander about.

He saw a shop called Falling Snow and stopped to check out the display window filled with snow globes. It was simple and clean with no signs. Snow globes with the Grand Hotel, the Mackinac Bridge, and even of the town.

Perfect. His niece collected snow globes and Beau brought her one back whenever he visited someplace interesting. He'd brought her one of the Golden Gate bridge and one of the Statue of Liberty. He'd also given her one of Jackson Square in New Orleans. This would complete one from each of the four corners of the country.

Unfortunately, it must be closed. The lights were off, but the sign on the door said it was open. Curious, he peeked into the shop. There was a young lady inside, but she was facing away from him. He knocked on the door. When she didn't hear, he cracked the door open and knocked again. "Hello. Are you open?"

She jumped and turned around, her smile troubled. "Yes. Please. Come in. We're just having a minor problem with the power."

He stepped inside, but it was really much too dark to see anything. "I can come back."

"No," she said quickly. "Please don't. I mean don't go. Do you have a penny?" She looked at him with hope splashed over her face. His heart did a little flip. It had taken him a minute, especially in the dim light, but he recognized her soft accent. She was from the south. Her features were soft, too. Her shoulder length brunette hair was tucked behind her unadorned ears.

He took another step closer, wanting to see her up close. Though he was drawn to her full pink lips, he stopped himself and focused on her question.

Beau didn't carry coins. He always had some cash for tips, but he never took the change. He shook his head.

Her smile vanished and she put a hand on her forehead.

"Why do you need a penny?"

"I can use it to fix the electricity."

Beau instantly knew what she was about. During high school, he'd worked with his father who was a contractor. His father had taught him anything he could ever want to know about electricity.

They'd once gone into an old house in Fort Worth. The house had to be completely rewired and Beau had done the whole thing himself. The older lady who lived there had pennies in each of the fuses. It was a wonder the place hadn't burned long before they'd been called in.

"You have a fuse box?" He closed the door and stepped toward her. Even in the dim light, he could see that the store sold nothing but snow globes. Another charming and unique thing on the island.

"Yes. And we're out of fuses." She walked closer and stepped into the sunlight that was coming in through the shop window.

He smiled. She was even more beautiful in the light. Her deep green eyes framed by lush black lashes sparkled. She immediately smiled back. The smile went to her eyes making her even more beautiful.

Suddenly three days was not nearly enough time.

Keep Reading Just Maybe.

ALSO BY KATHRYN KALEIGH

For a full and up-to-date list of Kathryn Kaleigh's books, visit www.kathrynkaleigh.com

Contemporary Romance

The Worthington Family

The Lady in the Red Dress

On the Edge of Chance

Sealed with a Kiss

Kiss me at Midnight

The Heart Knows

Billionaire's Unexpected Landing

Billionaire's Accidental Girlfriend

Billionaire Fallen Angel

Billionaire's Secret Crush

Billionaire's Barefoot Bride

The Heart of Christmas

The Magic of Christmas

In a One Horse Open Sleigh

A Secret Royal Christmas

An Old-Fashioned Christmas

Second Chance Kisses

Second Chance Secrets

First Time Charm

Three Broken Rules

Second Chance Destiny

Unexpected Vows

Begin Again

Love Again

Falling Again

Just Stay

Just Chance

Just Believe

Just Us

Just Once

Just Happened

Just Maybe

Just Pretend

Just Because

Time Travel Romance

Once Upon a Winter's Spell

THE BECQUERELS

Meet Me in 1879

Dragon's Blood

Lavender Blue

Champagne Silver

Twilight Frost

Mountbatten Pink

Written in the Wind

Scripted in the Stars

Destined in the Twilight

Promised in the Mist

Trapped in the Melody

Twist of Fate

When the Stars Align

Once in a Blue Moon

Once Upon a Christmas

A Wish Upon a Star

When Lightning Strikes

Storm of Time

Midnight Storm

When the Moon Falls

Stormborn Angel

Time Tempest

The Heart Remembers

A Moment in Time

Moonlight Shadows

Rescued in Time

Falling Through to Forever

HISTORICAL ROMANCE

Finding Natalie

Promising Samantha

Falling for Allyson

Saving Savannah

Claiming Charlie

Rescuing Kiera

Protecting Gabriella

Courting Isabella

Jasmine Kisses

Magnolia Kisses

Gardenia Kisses

Love Always

Beyond Enemy Lines

Hearts Under Siege

Hearts Under Fire

Wait for Me

Take Me Home

Keep Me Safe

Away Down South in Dixie

The Reluctant Bride

Stay with Me

Sign up for my newsletter at www.kathrynkaleigh.com to be the first to hear about new releases, as well as exclusive content, and more!

Kathryn Kaleigh writes sweet contemporary romance, time travel romance, and historical romance.

kathrynkaleigh.com